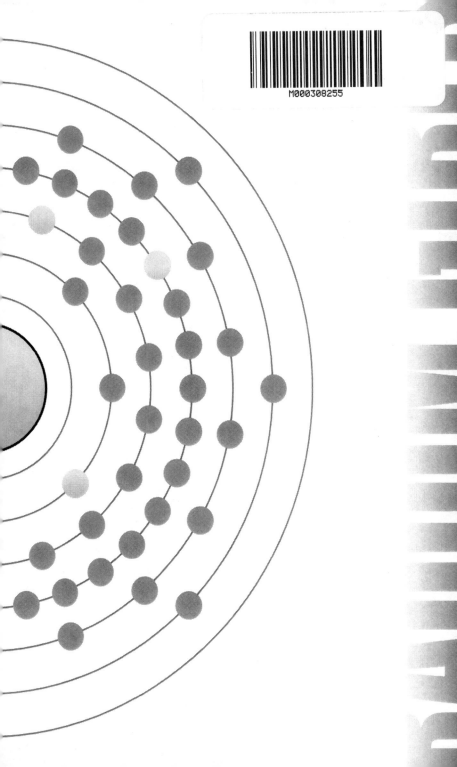

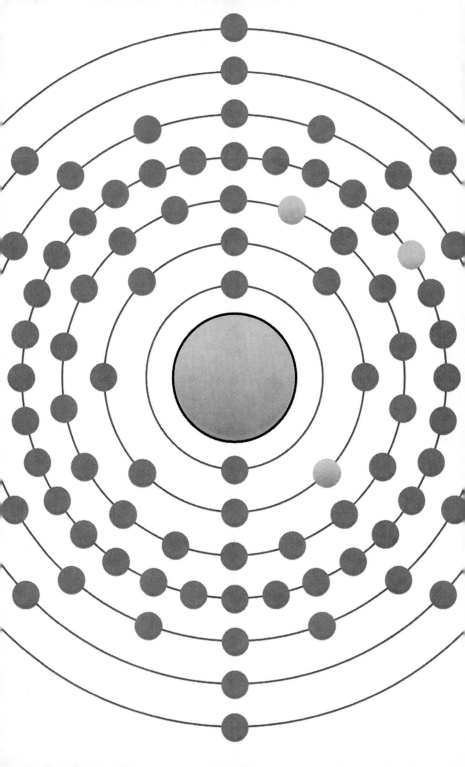

RADIUM GIRLS

by
Amanda Gowin

THUNDERDOME
PRESS

Radium Girls
c. 2014 Amanda Gowin
ISBN: 978-0692211687

Design, and Typesetting by Michael Paul Gonzalez

Printed and Bound by CreateSpace

Cover Design by Michael Paul Gonzalez

Interior Illustrations by Amanda Gowin

Zombie Hand illustration by Charles Hinds,
licensed through Creative Commons on DeviantArt

Eyeball illustration by Nikolina Ramljak,
licensed through Creative Commons on DeviantArt

This book will be released in electronic format, but its primary goal in design is to remind the reader of the simple pleasure of holding the printed work in hand. It's small enough to take with you to spread the word far and wide: the paper book is not dead.
Show it. Share it. Help it survive.

For Adam and Eric

Table of Contents

The Truth

To tell of magic and love and beauty in my past would be to tell secrets that are not just mine; the dewy grass at the edge of a tennis court under the full moon, flowers I stuffed in mailboxes at dawn, envelopes of poems left under my windshield wipers, afternoon light through the tin roof of a hayloft.

True things peek, they shove, they shape and tint. But here is fiction, with truth buried inside, and lies disguised as truths, and ugliness and beauty shaped by sleep and daydreams.

When reading this collection, if you think you see yourself, you probably do - or something you said, the way you looked, a conversation...

I am Dr. Frankenstein, and you gave me the pieces to make my monsters. Thank you for that.

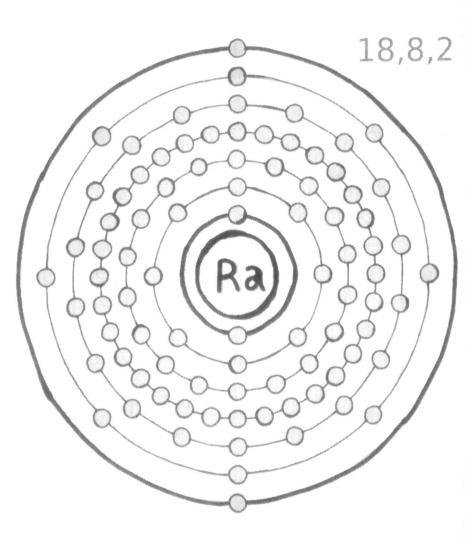

18,8,2

Radium is #88 on the Periodic Table. It glows in the dark, is beautiful and toxic, and will rot you to pieces with enough exposure. Never use it to brush your teeth.

HOLLOW CREATURES

A Play
by
Amanda Gowin &
H.R. Tardiff

RADIUM GIRLS

SETTING:	LIGHTS UP on a bare room. Pillows and tapestries litter the floor. CENTER are two wooden chairs, back to back, a large hookah between them.
AT RISE:	Seated on the chairs are AMANDA and HILARY, in silk dressing gowns, each with a mouthpiece in hand. They reach the end of a long, simultaneous exhale as lights reach full. A pause as the smoke rises.

                    AMANDA
It rained here for like five minutes. I
can see the air again. On my skin. The
dog is probably dead, he has fur.

                    HILARY
I had to freeze the house last night
to sleep. It was cold and humid and I
tossed and turned like an off-balance
washing machine. I think I finally fell
asleep when there were icicles on my
eyebrows. It was ludicrous.

RADIUM GIRLS

AMANDA

Icicles made of discontent. These are
the eyebrows of our discontent. My hair
is touching my neck but I broke the
clippers because my palms were sweaty
and now I can't even shave my head.

HILARY

My husband shaved my head for me last
time and now I'm ruined, that is, refuse
to do it myself. And music is going
really loud and my child is chanting
to her lid collection and the cicadas'
mating calls are still drowning out all
the pretty pretty noise in my head. I
swear to god, I am not running an insect
singles bar, they can all go home before
I napalm my lawn.

AMANDA

There's power when all the hair falls
on the floor and in the sink, reverse-
Samson for females, maybe. All the
cicadas here are made of electronic
things, they're metal and don't do that
rising hum, the purr that's supposed to
climax, crescendo, they just hum even
and on and on and on and on and never
pause to breathe because they can't
sweat, only rust; and how can they rust
if they don't sweat unless it rains? Not
the warm wet mist that recharges them
but the chilly icy kind that freezes
their insides, pops their gears.

HILARY

And they're desperate, because they were
born with a single purpose and the air
is thick and they can't pause to breathe
it or they will die. And they can't stop
the buzz or they will die. And they
can't go home, they can't find shelter
and they can't clean the rust in the
freezing water because if they fail, the
future is lost.
And there was something that happened, I
think, the first time someone shaved the
head of a woman and tried to take away
that power. No one really knows about
it, but every once in a while, someone
discovers it.

AMANDA

If you look in their eyes they're
shells already - that's why they're so
convincing - the machinery was pushed
in the abandoned shells with spiny,
jabby antennas pulled from the hoods
of the cars in nighttime parking lots,
just one hand reaching through the haze
and snapping them off, gathering a pile
like kindling, then holding the shells
carefully, one by one, inserting the
gears, tossing them in handfuls into the
sky knowing they'll float, slowly slowly
in the heavy air, between the heat and
the molecules and land on doorsteps and
leaves, clinging to screens.

HILARY

And they don't remember. Or maybe some
of them do. As they drifted through the
thick late summer air, both cold and
unbearably hot. They remember how the
life in their chests became a flicker
of electricity in their bellies and
they were meant to do nothing more than
just exist. And then the air, thick and
heavy, ground through the aching gears
in gasps and the floating somehow became
flight and they flew and flew until
their gasps became a buzz. And they
remembered.

AMANDA

And the woman was Rapunzel, there was no
witch, the prince shaved her head and
said 'There, I take your beauty and your
accessibility,' and she said 'Stupid,
now I am free,' and shoved him out the
window. She did not cry the eyes back
into his head where the thorns had taken
them, she said, 'Before you were blind
and now you can see...'

HILARY

The Prince survived, but never regained
his sight. Crippled and shamed. He
ordered his knights to climb the tower
and find the woman with no hair. For she
was fierce and dangerous and could not
be allowed freedom.

HILARY (Cont.)

And none of the knights returned and no one ever learned why. The tower became the standing monument to the Prince's failure. And so he had it taken down. And when the rubble littered the meadow where it had once stood so tall above the oaks and pines, he breathed a little easier, for surely she could not have escaped. But while he slept in his great castle, a woman watched him from the wall of his keep, a hood pulled tight around a shaven head. She smiled and used the walls and roofs to leave his kingdom.

AMANDA

And when he was sure, really sure she was dead, he forgot to sleep. When the winter ended and there were no more tracks for the hounds to follow, he spent the nights of spring wandering sleepless in the forests, listening for the lost knights, listening for her voice, forgetting time and forgetting eventually the possibility of her death. He wandered blind, hearing her voice around every corner, her footstep crunching a twig. His clothes were rags and his voice was hoarse and the kingdom forgot him, and death forgot him.

AMANDA (Cont.)

Mad, he collected the cicadas from trees
and carried them in his robes, to forget
her voice and drown her memory - and
time passed, and the hum died, and he
began to build the tiny machines, to
keep the possibility of Her forever at
bay....

HILARY

It is the legend of their buzz and
their ceaseless scream from the grass
and the weeds and thicker parts of the
forests. The hunger for something they
were intended to fulfill, but the scream
for something they can never have. It is
the legend that only a few know. Like
a mountain tale, whispered around the
fires and fading lanterns. Whispered and
quickly forgotten. And high above the
crumbling walls of his kingdom, above
the faded and forgotten banners of his
towers, the buzzing cicadas find a porch
surrounded by maples, thick with wind
chimes and blossoming mint and lavender.
A woman listens to their screams
piercing her windows. The sound pours
through the glass until it fills up the
walls of her home, the walls of her
head. She stands back from the mirror
and puts down the shears. The sound
pulls her, until finally she stands on
her porch, in the dense humid air of
late summer.

LIGHTS FADE TO BLACK

AS INSECTS SING

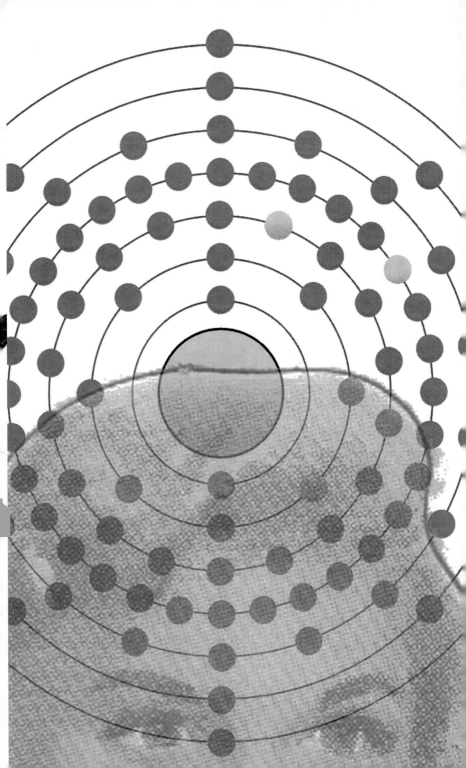

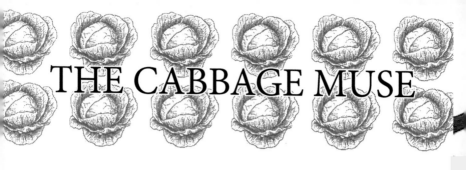

THE CABBAGE MUSE

Does your grandmother grow cabbage?

Not a question that would normally draw a seventeen year old from a packaging glitch that opened up no less than twelve channels of honest-to-goodness hardcore porn - acts of debauchery Jonah was sure dated back to mysterious drawing boards scribbled by the incestuous and bastard children of P.T. Barnum and the Marquis de Sade that were educated solely by pages of the Kama Sutra fed through the bars of their cages -

His boner took down an empty soda bottle and a sheath of scribbled pen and ink figures as he scrambled for the firefly light of the phone. Backlit by orange-tan breasts too new to bounce, the papers settled in a circle around his feet and he tapped the magic light that read CECILIA.

Do you have a cabbage patch?

Are you fucking with me? Is this about fucking? Thumbs flying, eyes darting from large screen to small screen.

I need to know who I'm going to marry. I need to find a cabbage patch.

Where are you?

Answer the fucking question.

The moon was a crooked yellow grin outside the window.

He blackened the T.V. and typed. *My uncle Dave.*

Zipping his jeans proved difficult. Shoes were evasive in the near dark, and Cecilia blinked like a steady heartbeat while he tangled the laces into something mimicking bows.

I'm at the end of the road. I was gonna throw rocks at your window but you were watching people fuck and I didn't want to embarrass you so I went back to the car.

A moan escaped him, not unlike those from the forgotten porn, and Jonah crept down the stairs and out a kitchen door which proved too sympathetic to creak.

Dew hissed a warning as he cut a path through the grass, leaving a dark trail behind him. He stuck close to the house until cover disappeared, and resisted the urge to run. Jonah planted his Chucks in the gravel with the sound of fireworks but paced himself. He would walk to Cecilia. Not run.

September threatened to be nothing but a fever dream. Jonah was probably flipping in his August sheets, sweaty with chattering teeth - imagining Cecilia next to her Dad's El Camino, barefoot in the dark, phone dangling at the end of one long arm, dark hair in a tight knot on top of her head, skin glowing, grinning like the moon.

"How long you back?"

"Till they catch me. Tomorrow at the latest, they have all these GPS things and I don't know what works and what doesn't or how to turn them off. The car doesn't, but my phone probably does. Fuck it. You look good," Cecilia circled him, quiet and feline. Her dress was white, it floated around her. None of this was happening.

"So do you. Pincushion queen. Where's the blonde?"

"It was making me hyper. Get in the car, we have to find cabbage stalks. I can't take the suspense any longer."

The dash lights lit her like the dead. Cheekbones and glass eyes. Jonah's jeans were uncomfortably tight. The car walked the broken glass of the gravel to the pavement and made a familiar right under her knuckles.

Bent from his pocket, Jonah straightened two Camels and popped the lighter. She jumped at the noise. "I don't want to know anything," he offered quietly with the lit cigarette.

Cecilia laughed, but the roundness of her eyes became less pronounced. She wet her bottom lip and took the cigarette with her mouth, brushing his fingertips. "You need to know more about fortune-telling. We have to -"

"Left on Horton Sisters."

"I remember!" The car swung, creating a private gravity within as it fishtailed and kicked up gravel dust.

"Sure you do."

"Dukes of Hazzard is the only way to drive a car like this. If we make it to morning we should take it to the strip mines."

Smoke filled the car. Stratus clouds. Jonah melted into the door, watched her breathe, watched her smoke, watched her purse her lips, watched her be. In all the world – or county – Cecilia had chosen him. Over and over, she chose him, whipping into town for One Night Only.

"Second right." He flicked the butt and left the window cranked down. "What the fuck are we doing?"

"Determining my future. I swear to god I didn't make it up, it was in a book. The moon is waxing. This is when we're supposed to do it."

"Fuck?"

Her cheeks colored and his chest ached.

"Here – just pull off here," Jonah directed them to a soft spot at the edge of the road.

The headlights gave up about two feet into the fog. Cecilia killed the engine but not the lamps. "I know about my name. Not just yours. You have to escape the whale. Cecilia is a muse. I just have to exist. Did you know that?"

Jonah did, but her eyes were too expectant to disappoint. "No." His arm was out, hand almost to her throat, and she turned and kicked open the door.

"That's why we're here!" Cecilia bolted into the fog, sure in the furrow as a tightrope walker.

Gone.

The keys hung from the ignition, Jonah hung in space. Stuffing found his fingers, bursting from the cracks in the leather. He didn't wake up, and she didn't return, so he pocketed the keys and followed her into the cabbage field.

Lightning bugs were sparse, shutting down for the night. Each breath drew in fog, and his sneakers slipped and fumbled where her toes had been. The prints were distinct and sure. In the coming days he could bring plaster, fill them and make sets of Cecilia prints, lay them in a circle around his bed.

"Jonah!"

"Cecilia?"

"It's you!"

"Of course it's -" he began, but realized in whatever bizarre ritual she had just performed, she meant: It's YOU.

Consequences were for those without magic, not those who stood in the fog under the moon, lungs empty, mere feet from a pale creature in a translucent gown. Cecilia floated on her toes, ankles crossed, brandishing a soddy cabbage stalk like a head, or a rabbit from a hat.

The battery was dead and the marriage unconsummated in the barely-dawn when the red and blue lights from her daddy's cruiser filled the El Camino's interior, but for Jonah, nothing felt unfinished. She was gently unwound from her tangled rest in his arms – a half-sleeping rag doll with a wide and understanding gaze - displaced but not unhappy. Cecilia waved goodbye and knuckled her eyes, tethered to her father's hand and led away like a precocious child.

The Sheriff nodded to him without prejudice. He wrapped the seventeen year old in his coat. Jonah watched him talk her into slippers large as clown shoes while the morning crept up and the Deputy jumped the El Camino. With any luck Deputy Henley'd drop him off before his grandmother was out out of bed.

He toed the cabbage stalk in the floorboard and the hoods slammed. The perfect imprint of her ear lay on the inside of his forearm, a Golden Spiral . The cruiser's taillights disappeared and he wondered when she would again appear, and who she would be.

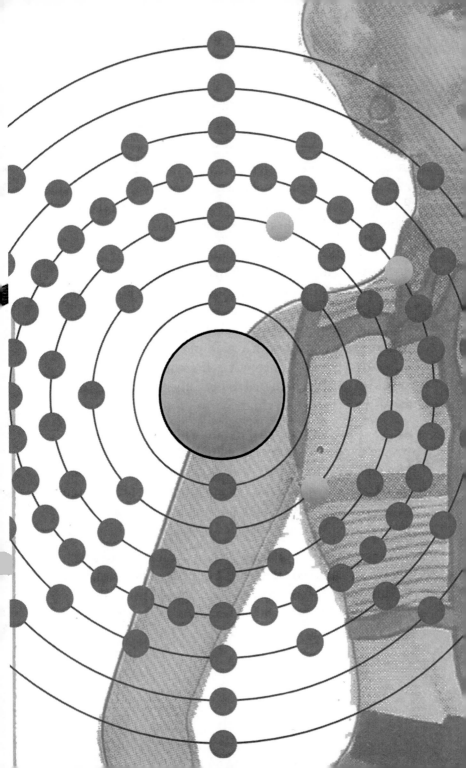

TEETOTALER

Kathy's jaw clicks with each clench on her nicotine gum - a rapid double barrel noise.

Squish-snap. Squish-snap. Squish-snap.

Add the erratic flicker of an overhead fluorescent on the fritz and you've got the saddest nightclub simulation Nathan has ever experienced. He's on day four hundred and forty-one. His fingers lock on a dangerously full Styrofoam cup, he manages not to crush it and spill lukewarm sludge all over his hands and the sad linoleum. To do so would be to interrupt, to trivialize the words that spill from the current sharer's tear-stained face.

And Nathan would never do that, especially not to Gerald. Gerald is bald and forty and fat and stopped drinking a day late. The others in the sad circle of folding chairs are learning:

"She gave me a month," Gerald's head gleams, hands dangling between his knees, "but I blew it off. She wasn't lying." First time to speak in fourteen weeks, and Gerald spills it. She left with full suitcases. He followed, banged on her elderly mother's door - called them cunts and cursed his (now) ex-wife's barren womb - vomited in the lawn and said if they had kids he wouldn't drink. It was her fault, her fault, he'd said -

Normally an avid and sympathetic listener, on this particular Tuesday evening Nathan listens with one melodramatic ear - the other is full of Kathy's nervous chomping. A sideways glance at her, shuffling his feet, but she won't look over. The gum pops and snaps erratically, then her jaw commences rhythm at double speed.

Guilty, guilty, guilty. Kathy's off the wagon and she doesn't want to tell. It's only been five weeks since her tacky skirts began spreading over the metal seats, and she broke her promise. Breathalyzer tube in her car and she broke her promise. Drove through her neighbor's yard and over their cat, and she broke her promise.

And there she sits - Squish-snap. Squish-snap - because she knows that Nathan knows. Bitch wouldn't say a word, wouldn't blink at her hypocrisy if he hadn't slid into the chair next to her. If he hadn't busted her. Has everything she said been a lie, besides the fact that she was court-ordered to attend? He's hated her always, hates her fat ankles and the discreet way she glances at her watch during prayer.

Five fucking weeks, and she wouldn't say a word or even have the decency to look distressed if she hadn't been caught.

Nathan kept boxes under his bed, boxes of pictures and scraps of material to remind him why he quit. He lays in the dark with the half-open blinds slicing him into uncertain pieces, remembering that drunk girls laughed if you bit them on the shoulder in a public place. With alcohol, every body part gleamed and expected to be touched. Clothes practically fell off, consent was variable. Boxes under his bed so he would remember, so he would remember consent was NOT variable. Keep your hands to yourself. Stay out of bars. Stay out of convenience stores after dark.

Those boxes - his increasing inability to blanket his guilt, to rest above his reminders, his legacy, his insurance against falling off the wagon - were the reason he started roaming.

Day three hundred and ninety-two, he'd started walking the nights away. Shouldering through laughing groups of girls, chin to his chest, hands in pockets. The ghost of his face reflected back in the windows of pubs. His heart thumping, out of sync from the steady rhythm of bass from the clubs he passed.

Nathan could stay out, but he couldn't stay away.

Streetlights throwing circles in the dark, he began to measure progress from circle to circle as much as day by day. Jack the Ripper fog clung to him from summer into autumn, a cloak of guilt; still he walked.

The reliable click of his own footsteps was the very reason for Kathy's distress.

Day four hundred and thirty-eight, Nathan's soles were nearly worn through as the sidewalk ate his shoes. Four hundred and thirty-eight days, the boxes under his bed struggling against him, turning to dreams instead of nightmares. Four hundred and thirty-eight days, he plowed into Kathy as she came out of a corner dive, hard enough to knock her drunken frame off balance and flat on her back on the concrete.

"Jesus Christ!" she shrieked as she pushed herself upright, hair in her eyes and one shoe gone.

He'd put out his hand to help her to her feet, answering quietly, "No, just Nathan, Kathy. But if you feel like hearing a bad joke: I could arrange for you to meet him." Wide smile.

The bitch was drunk enough to laugh, and dumb

enough to take his hand. Nathan hauled her up, the first time he'd felt the weight of a human against him in four hundred and thirty-eight days.

"I think you broke my ass," she slurred, audacious enough to grin mischievously while she struggled into her black high heel. "Think there's a crack in it."

Nathan let her go, all thirty-odd years of her wasted breath, wide ass, unlovable and very warm body. Kathy had emerged alone, and it was close to 2am.

"I've never really looked at you before," she said. "You're tall - and a lot younger than I thought."

He replied, "I've been told I'm all hands and eyes." No one else on the street. Faint honky-tonk beyond the door, she'd fallen through like a last-minute gift.

Lipstick gone, eyeliner smeared, dignity nowhere to be found, Kathy pushed her hair back from her eyes and blinked faux-Bette Davis. "I've had quite a bit to drink, Nathan. Do you think you could take me home?"

Polaroids of breasts and hands tucked into boxes under his bed. Painfully clean, painfully lonely apartment. Liquor stores closed, but there were other ways to skin a cat.

A cat. Day four hundred and thirty-eight. He blinked and frowned at her, disgusted. "There's a dead cat in the alley over there. Round as a balloon. Remind you of where you should be Tuesday night? Want to come with me to look, poke it with a stick? Bet it pops."

"Fuck you. What are you gonna do, tattle? Who the fuck are you? You're not even my sponsor." Kathy swung her purse, backing away, nearly losing her balance.

He threw a longing glance into the alley - those

little pockets of dark, designed for secrecy, rape, drug deals, the popping of cat carcasses, all forms of deviance - and sighed. "No. I'll give you the chance to tell on yourself." His shoulders folded against her gaze as he turned; she might have called after him.

Day four hundred and forty-one.

Squish-snap. Squish-snap.

Nathan's sponsor Gerald has long since dried his eyes, and fifteen people who are trying their damned best - plus Kathy - say goodbyes, gathering empty cups and jackets.

"Thanks for not ratting me out," a voice in his ear, and Kathy clinks her folded chair into his in the row along the wall. Nathan looks up blankly. Shakes his head.

"Not my job," he answers. Stabbing his arms into his long coat, he snatches hers off the rack. "Walk you home?"

The space between themselves and the bright light of the YMCA grows. At the crosswalk he stops abruptly. Ahead, the rings of the streetlights stretch in a perfectly feasible path to...

Path to...?

Wrinkling his eyebrows, Nathan veers right, Kathy with him. They walk in silence for perhaps five minutes while he takes odd lefts and rights into darker and darker streets, past the bars, past barking dogs. Kathy's lack of hesitation is her certainty they're going back to his place to fuck: she's matched her footsteps to his.

"To be perfectly honest, I really don't get this whole AA thing," she finally begins, laughing.

He locks a hand around her upper arm and ducks into the alley to their right, heart in his throat, dragging her with him. Her bone twists beneath the flesh, he presses her against the wall. Dirty wall. Rougher than sandpaper, more interesting in its variability. Broken glass under their feet, recognizable by the teeth-grinding scrape it makes on the asphalt. Thumb and forefinger working into her grimace, he drags the slimy wad of strawberry-stinking gum from between her teeth and flattens it onto the wall.

"I do," Nathan whispers into her mouth. Sometimes the thing you love most in the world is the one thing you should avoid at all costs, because it's bad for you, bad for others - but it still feels better than anything. So you need to be around people that understand that feeling, to know you are not alone, that every day you have to remind yourself why you don't give in.

Unbuttoning her blouse rapidly, other hand around her throat, Nathan is suddenly uncertain what he has shared and what has been inner monologue. Her pulse jumps beneath his thumb. He doesn't remember slipping on the gloves.

And that there are other people fighting just as hard if not harder than you. Nathan cannot see her face in the dark and does not want to. He hates her face. It's a lie.

"Four hundred and forty-one days. I burned the boxes under the bed Saturday night after I saw you. But I told myself if you confessed, if you would just try, I would let it go." He shapes his mouth carefully to be sure he voices this.

A choked sob escapes her with a waft of strawberry, and he removes his hand. "I'll still tell," she hisses hopefully. "Next week. Next week - or - or right now. Not everyone is gone. We can go back. I can start over. I can start over tonight."

The tone of voice so familiar, the words don't matter. Always the strained calm, the assurance of whatever is needed to make him stop. Knees weak, he places his hand carefully back over her windpipe. No reason to explain he was on the fence already - that no matter how fast or how far he walks, how many streetlight paths he follows, he still needs the alleys. Still needs the flutter and the struggle. Running into her - literally - on Saturday had been the last sign. "I just need a little break," he mumbles. She begins to cry, but he continues. "The important thing to remember is that I can start over."

In the dark, in the alley, under the faraway moon, the smell of piss and rot nearly make him cry with the sense of home. The familiar last ditch flailing of Her. All these things must be what the others feel when they slip into a bar. Climb onto a stool. Watch the bartender touch the neck of the bottle to the lip of the glass, gently, gently.

Shot glass reaching the mouth. Needle piercing the vein. Penis touching just the edge of the vaginal lips, almost, almost. Quarter half in the slot machine.

The firm handle under his gloved palm, the upward thrust of the blade, slipping through her skin and upward under her sternum, delicious resistance and a completely unique slurping, tearing sound. Her body stiffens and Nathan covers her mouth smoothly to stifle the scream of pain and surprise. Takes two steps back with a dancer's fluid movement to keep the blood from pouring onto his shoes.

She shakes, bleeding out, body vibrating against his fist, under his palm. Burying his face in the shoulder of her jacket, Nathan cries with happiness and despair. Cries with relief.

An hour later he is still walking, fingering the Polaroids deep in his pocket. He will not look at them, at the ghost illuminated.

Dropping his gloves into a trash can as he passes, Nathan finds the circles of streetlights that lead home. More ashamed by the stillness inside than failure, he sets his worn soles back on the path.

Tomorrow is Day One.

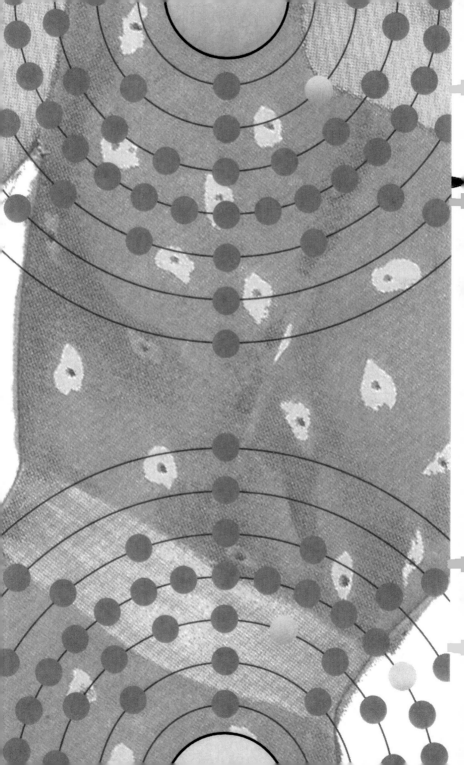

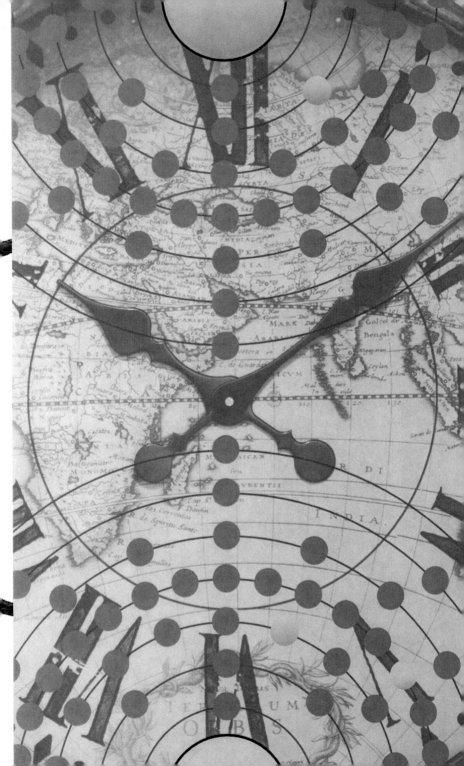

THE WORLD WAS CLOCKS

Descending the staircase as one, four legs in perfect time, the light was blue on four black braids.

Clasped hands parted with an electric pop as Tilly paused on a creaking stair. Her knuckles whitened on the rail. Rocking, she repeated the offending creak. Her eyes widened, cheeks reddened.

Tabitha, one stair lower and suddenly one plane removed, widened her eyes and laid a hand to her cheek. Nothing.

Tilly said: "One day this place will fall in, and I will not be under it."

Symmetry disappeared.

Tabitha scratched the palm of her hand, scratched the itch of a phantom limb to see Tilly's half of the room stripped bare the following morning.

The oak tap-tapped at the window in sympathetic Morse code, but the sun and tree were too bright to be trusted. Finding Tilly's imprint on the bare mattress, she folded herself against the light and pressed the concavity of her sister. What tomb?

Sixteen years old, Tabitha was astounded at the world through one set of eyes. Pausing on the judge and jury stair, her parents' twinspeak crept up to her, peppered with words and phrases for the first time.

Tabitha stepped into their world.

A faded set? She stared. At five, the twins smiled from the sandbox and the mommy and daddy smiling down were vivid and flushed with youth.

Suddenly time was everything.

"I must acclimate myself into this world," she whispered into the mirror, into Tilly.

Forehead to the cool glass she remembered their hatred for Alice—Alice didn't know. On the other side was another—where else would a twin come from? There had been much debate as to who belonged to this world, and who had daringly climbed in.

The tears her reflection gave back were a comfort until breath obscured the face in fog.

Tabitha pressed, but the glass did not yield.

Ill-equipped, with naked eyes and thoughts, school whipped around her in a flurry of bodies, voices, and bells. Without Tilly the world was clocks. They hovered with round faces and she scurried away from their pointing hands.

"Their world."

Other girls began to fascinate Tabitha. Peering from around her melancholy, studying them, a picket fence of red lockers lit a vertical path to the circle they made.

Deep breath and sense of falling, one big step. Surrounded. She searched the eyes of a redhead, murmured into the ear of a brunette, smiled at a dark girl so different and perfect as to almost be unreal—this girl flushed and broke her gaze.

"We are—no, I am beautiful," she told her

conspirator in the long bedroom mirror.

Late nights in cars drinking gin from the bottle with a shy blonde who had never done this sort of thing. Tabitha kissed the girl's palm and placed it flush with hers, admiring the differences.

The ghost of Tilly itched and Tabitha cried, palms pressed to their cold reflections in the mirror, an aura of moisture welding them.

Tabitha blinked, the bell of her skirt had paced her. She opened her eyes and high school was over, the girls disappeared. Again, she was expected to recreate the whole world.

Tabitha studied her parents—aged turtle doves—and envied their stasis.

She discovered males.

Clumsy and oppressive, they lacked softness. But she rested in the crooks of their arms while they confessed the same fears as the delicate girls she had loved.

And what was love? Yellow urine on a stick turning pink, pails of blue paint obliterating the room she and Tilly had known. Her parents asked who it belonged to, their brows furrowed.

"Me," Tabitha answered, puzzled, hands on her warm belly.

She grew fat as the tree out her window unfolded tiny green hands. Love was color in the world. Her laughter drew laughter from the mouths and eyes of her parents— rusty notes that became well-oiled and silver, and came easily. Tabitha browned in the sun.

Her reflection no longer resembled Tilly's. The mounting wire snapped as she took the mirror from the wall, and mourning for her twin ceased.

Movement and rush, laughter and tears as they piled in the car. Headlights slicing through the sheets of rain, tiny green suitcase on her lap, Tabitha was too happy to scream.

Palms flat on on the suitcase of carefully folded nightgowns and handmade baby clothes, and two worn bears exactly the same.

Color grows slowly but disappears in an instant— in a click of teeth hard enough to make the tongue bleed. Alone in the hospital, the color and motion were sucked away into the fluorescent lights above, leaving only the drone of the doctor's voices.

Tabitha remembered nothing but the taste of pennies. She woke from the dream into this ugly grey world to hear about 'the accident' from a stranger. A story as preposterous as the TV ones her mother watched in the afternoons.

"So I dreamed it all?" She saw only her suitcase, tiny and insignificant in the corner.

The doctor didn't understand.

"Where's Tilly?"

All efforts to reach her sister had been unsuccessful...

Rolling to the wall, the better to forget the little suitcase, she cried without the comfort even of a mirror.

The clocks stopped, or spun backwards and forwards in apathetic bursts. The lights marked a forgotten pattern, off and on. Beeping machines, murmurs from the hallway. Scratchy, drab sheets around her and under her hands. Interrogations were called 'evaluations.' Armed with clipboards and scowls, white coats floated in like vultures, made their faces into question marks and scratched at their boards before leaving.

Finally, the word she longed to hear: Release.

The sad box of a room ejected her. A woman with careful hands tucked her into a car and followed familiar roads. 'Social worker' the woman was called.

Tabitha rubbed her eyes, waking, planted in the living room with the suitcase at her feet.

Not one clock dared tick.

The house was a tomb.

No pain in the crescents her nails made in her palms, but the rage was consuming. She dragged all the mirrors into the painted room. Her father's hammer was found on the porch rail, laid to rest after hanging a wind chime from the rafter. She gripped the handle tightly as dragonflies spun and tinkled, leaving spots in her eyes.

Her heart swelled. Running up the stairs, the fateful step creaked and she released a howl that scratched her throat in its escape, blurred her vision, but did not slow her ascent. She raised the hammer, watched by a thousand overlapping Tillys and Tabithas, and did not put it down until the pieces were too small to reflect.

Yawning, she dismantled things little by little to know she was awake. Time was marked by Social Worker's visits—the woman arrived periodically to wear a face both worried and confused.

Mainly it was the dolls that worried Social Worker.

The project had been time-consuming—taking them apart and hanging the pieces by bright skeins in the branches of the big tree.

Social Worker warned about the group home.

The dolls belonged to the twins, their mother had dragged them from the attic back in the time of Tabitha's swollen belly. Discovering them in a sad pile on her parents' bed, she remembered the chaplain at the hospital saying her baby had gone into the sky. It was comforting. She mimicked it the only way she knew.

Sometimes when the wind blew, the plastic arms knocked together and she thought of babies clapping, and the dragonfly wind chime gave up a few rusty notes. For a moment her heart was light and so was the world, for a moment there was color, faint hues of blue and gold in the sky, blue in the dolls' eyes.

What could it matter to the warm body whose job was only to see that she was eating and keeping herself clean? Turning her head, Social Worker eventually went away again.

Falling, change, upside down, all these words were forgotten.

One day a taxicab appeared, an improbability so far from town, and crunched to a stop in a cloud of gravel dust. She rose—the porch swing gave a perfect view, but she did not believe.

From the cloud emerged Tilly, suitcase in hand. On her hip balanced a birdlike child of perhaps two, black hair and round eyes.

Tilly shuffled down the walk, head down, steps deliberate. The child's eyes flickered back and forth between the twins and her mouth made a perfect O, asking, "Who?"

"Tabitha," Tilly said in both answer and greeting, dropping the suitcase. Her eyes flitted over the tree.

"What's her name?" Tabitha's voice was a croak.

"Don't know. Won't tell me, won't answer to anything." A single braid snaked over Tilly's shoulder, scars zigzagged the arm enfolding the child. "Where are the others?"

"Dead."

Tilly nodded. "I'll come in and never leave again."

"No."

"I'll come in anyway." With sad eyes she plodded up the porch steps.

The little girl put out both arms and Tabitha wrapped her up, the weight comfortable against her, warmth unfamiliar. Tiny fingers linked behind her neck. The screen door slammed behind all of them and Tabitha's limbs tingled. The nameless child dropped to her bare feet and scrambled under the kitchen table.

"Can I stay in our room?" Tilly asked.

"It's not ours."

Tabitha watched her sister—Tilly's eyes swallowed every change, her hand fluttered over the stair rail.

The rattle of pans, crack of eggs, sizzle of bacon failed to draw the girl out. Tabitha fought the feeling of waking up, stirred and turned and blinked. She felt the child watching.

"What's your name?" Tabitha asked.

"Tabitha." A heart-shaped face appeared between the chair legs. Blue eyes. Voice like a bell, a wind chime.

"Yes. What's your name?"

"Tabitha."

Tilly reappeared at the foot of the stairs, pale.

Bending, Tabitha asked, "Will you be Tabby? We can't both be Tabitha."

"I Tabitha." Unblinking. She looked at the twins.

"Will you be Tabby?" Tilly asked.

Tabitha shrugged.

The afternoon passed untying the pieces from the tree. The yard became a giant chessboard of slowly reassembling dolls.

Tabitha looked up, her twin was gone.

The little girl wandered the rows of fragments, a plastic arm in hand.

Searching room to room, Tabitha finally stopped at the doorway she had not crossed in years.

The broken glass had disappeared, the wood floor glowed bright honey. The cradle in the corner was empty, and the curtains reached inwards, offering their wispy shadows.

Shaking, she climbed through the open window onto the roof.

Tilly stood near the chimney, hair loose and blown into the exact shape of a gingko leaf.

Urn in one hand, lid in the other.

Approaching carefully, quietly, Tabitha extended a spidery arm to meet her sister's.

The metal container was the size and heft of a baby bottle when she wrapped her clammy fingers around it. Before thinking twice, Tabitha flipped her wrist and swung her arm in a wide arc, tearing a gash in time and space.

A rainbow of ashes caught in the wind, tossed into the branches of the tree. Rustling leaves spread them further. Some drifted into the old sandbox, but that was okay.

Below, the child Tabitha saw the twins on the roof, jumped up and down, and clapped her hands.

Color the suitcase blue!

TINDER BOX

One can endure a snowy night for a long time, pressing bare fingers into melting patterns on the rails, pressing bare feet into a walked-along shape of sprawling tree that covers the length of the porch. Sometimes the blowing flakes throw shadows the size of fifty cent pieces down over one's pajamas, changing a person to a disco ball in reverse. Even after appendages are numb, one can light another cigarette for spite and blow smoke into the face of the moon.

The monster in the house is the monster I made.

Often, insanity lies dormant, wooed to sleep with an orderly life and emotional detachment, locked up in the place that also holds the capacity to love and fear. Then a girl may come along, a girl with bony arms and a lot of teeth that smokes too many Marlboros, and her scent, her pheromones, her voice and clicking shoes invade: snake in the sleeping monster's nose and throat and eyes, over and through the vines that wind around the box where Important Things are kept. The vines tingle sleeping limbs awake, the lock hisses and cracks, the box yawns, and inside, a heart beats.

But one cannot wake just the beautiful parts. Everything precious is stashed together - the heart and the weakness and the fists and the guns and the childhood slights and the bitterness of unrequited love from kindergarten onward, the sound of laughter from mocking children, the scratched-off faces of action figures in a shoebox, all of these things are freed, they flood the stomach and boil up to the soft palate, and True Love is conceived, steeped in bile and doubt, discolored with old bruises.

One cannot reach into Pandora's Box just for peppermint candy, the stench of corpses leaves an aftertaste.

His breath tastes of cocaine drip and Nazi medals, but mine tastes of cigarettes and is unacceptable.

One can stand on a snowy porch alone with purple hands and feet, knowing approximately how long it takes for him to become distracted, how long to wait before asking to be let back inside, where it's warm and orange and the pistol grips are always damp and the knives are always being cleaned and the monster speaks in movie lines while cutting lines because there's a twelve year old that's been loosed who still wants so badly to be cool, and the bathroom locks from the outside and the phone's been disconnected and a sneeze on a mirror is enough to...

Next door in the duplex is a young minister and his wife. One can stare at that door for hours, it will never open. Why knock, when the walls are paper thin and they know there's a girl locked outside in the snow? They have done nothing nothing nothing, never peeked or called, and I'll never knock, never, never, and I hate them and hate their God, the god that says turn up the television and turn off the porch light. I flick my cigarette onto their welcome mat.

One becomes comfortable in fear, wears it like a coat sewn of bloody mink pelts and obligation to stave off hypothermia. Soon I will leave him to fend for himself, tear off this skin with teeth and WWII memorabilia, leave him with nothing to feed on.

But tonight the moon is icy indifference.

Tonight my mouth tastes of pennies.

Tonight this coat is slick with blood and fits too well.

I tap at his door with blue knuckles.

What would the mat
outside your door say?

FEVER

Discipline, geometry, timing, and rhythm.

Charlotte undoes her tight French braid, finger over finger. Mouth set, she tucks her chin and yells from beneath her veil of hair, "Run it from the top!"

The first notes of Elvis's version of *Fever* bleed from the walls, top volume. Right hip locks with the blue light every second flash of the fixed strobe pattern. Three lights: blue, red, purple. White spotlight for new girls, they work under a fixed, merciless circle, hesitation their selling point.

Stock still except for the hip, rolling the flesh and bone outward. Forward step, discard the blue, left leg hyper-extends into purple. Legs together, head forward, arms at sides, hips thrusting slowly through the rest of the bass intro.

Possessed. Think possessed. Let the music in you. Count of four before the horns crash, toss back the hair and breasts forward into the red -

Purple!

"Can we start over? I fucked up."

"Dammit , Charlotte," the voice of God or the Wizard of Oz replaces Elvis. "I gotta piss. Take five and remember you got forty minutes."

"Thanks Jim," Reaching for the bottle of water, she almost snags it. Overheads kick on and stun, she bumps it with blind fingertips, hearing it roll slowly off the edge.

If this were a more romantic life, less about geometry and lighting and money, a hand would stop the bottle's descent from the honey-colored stage before it hit the sticky floor.

One bounce and it thumps a table leg. Fuck it. Charlotte's not touching anything on that floor. Slippers and robe on a chair beside the gleaming and overrated pole, she dresses and hops out of the light.

Humming, Violet AKA Cindy is spread over a bar stool in full make-up. She's one of two new girls, with the rhythm of an elephant on cough syrup, but her tits are the size of water melons - no one will notice her legs, her destiny is up-tempo. "When you do it, it looks like Fosse," she passes Charlotte a lit cigarette ringed in purple gloss and lights another for herself. "When I do it, it's like the bonobo mating dance."

"Were you counting? How did I miss the red for the horns? That's the place to hit the red, and I think I'll just have him cut the other colors after that. Makes sense, right?" No reason to compare and contrast their methods, she reasons. Pick a thing and do it perfectly - if you can't, slice off your fingertips and pick something else. One long pull on the cigarette, there's no mingling of colors on the butt, Charlotte never paints for blocking.

Poor Cindy has the shit shift, doing her monkey shake for the after-work-or-in-between-planes crowd.

Early afternoon light sneaks through an open service door and Cindy's eyes look vampiric, almost comical. The red stool where she perches is too red; there's too much gold on the walls. The plum carpet is worn and stained. Charlotte has crow's feet. Jim slips past, back to the sound booth, just a middle-aged guy with male-pattern baldness and a son overseas. Pay no attention to that man behind the curtain.

But when the lights dim, the waitresses shimmy and the girls undress, this place will look just right: mysterious, glittering, just out of reach. Things kittens bat at, things men jerk off to.

"Charlotte, you a go?" Oz, the Great and Terrible.

"On my way!" Thirty-five minutes before the doors cave inward and Violet skips onto the stage, lollipop and all. Charlotte leans in. "Cindy, you're gonna do fine - fuck the other girl, you'll open for me Saturday, I'd bet your red bonobo ass on it. Starla is a B cup and a prima-donna, you can't be both. You know what her real name is?"

Head tilted, eyes hopeful, Cindy answers, "No."

"None of us do! She says 'Starla' all the time will be just fine. And she asked Tim for my Valentine show spot, wanted to do a scarf dance to Beethoven. What the fuck does she know about Beethoven?" She grinds her cigarette in a tin tray. "You know, we should do an Oz number. I'd be the Tin Man, you'd be Dorothy."

"Charlotte." Tim says.

Cindy's mouth turns at the corners, down then up. "Thanks. I got student loans, you know. You're like a beautiful fucking snake or a butterfly or something."

Before she receives a kiss or hug or gets any form of stripper glitter or smell on her, Charlotte darts between the round tables and hoists herself over the lip of the stage.

Her mom said all that shit about doing things perfectly or doing something else - not the fingerprint bit, though, Charlotte added that herself.

Sitting more upright than her bench, her mother French braided her hair, the surety of each movement imprinted into Charlotte's scalp. The piano keys always gleamed, that's what threw her off – mashing her dirty fingers all over such pristine bone and ebony.

The last day she played, sixteen and pale and perfect, the music flowed through her. Best day of her life. Red hearts and flowers blossomed; music dripped between the keys. The white became pink and slippery. Charlotte fumbled notes and stumbled through one last melody. She drifted away lightheaded, beaten, conquered, satisfied.

"Go for it!" Charlotte calls, and shuts her eyes. Bass rolling like waves, her hip catches the blue light, lets it go, catches it again. She finds the purple and the snare, waiting for the red.

GILDED BONES

Flat on my back, legs up, with one foot on either side of a framed photo of a red pomeranian, I can't help but wonder if it looks as if I've birthed a wall of these monsters.

Slick plywood disguised as cedar paneling is cool against blistered heels. It smells of dog and pet stain remover here. There are twelve fox-faced puffballs staring down at me.

The blood's all in my head from lying half upside down.

Maybe I did splatter these walls with fluff and gnashing teeth and yipping. If not, I certainly was the enabler.

Twelve tiny skeletons are buried in the crawl space beneath the trailer.

I've been home too long.

Celeste wanted Hollywood – or Vegas. To her there was no difference. Razzle dazzle and lipstick, high heels and black sunglasses. Round beds occupied by celebrities, sunshine and shrimp platters. Glamour pets and thin legs. Opportunity in every set of male eyes that fell on her neckline.

Gold.

A life of panning for gold. California doesn't really change.

The botched suicide disappointed her. She smoked long cigarettes while ghosts with clipboards and stethoscopes floated past the door and waited for her to bleed out - or cough, and end it fast. There had been no blood-splattered walls, no dramatic black and white crime scene photos. No detectives had shaken their heads at the waste of a perfectly fuckable woman caught in harsh flashbulbs, an old photo of the Hollywood First National Building clutched in her left fist.

She got a bullet that couldn't be moved and a ticking clock.

Turns out, closest the bitch got to the west coast was knocked up in Indiana, nineteen years old stripping at a place called Tammy's until she started to show, and the manager – most likely my real dad – gave her money for a bus ticket back to Ohio.

The last day she said, "You know, the worst thing that can happen somewhere like L.A. is you get cut in half and become a national treasure or mystery or whatever, or some psycho leaves pieces of you in dumpsters or something and tracks animal prints in blood patterns around the drop spots."

"Never heard about anything like that, animal prints." I snaked a cigarette from her silver case.

She'd shrugged. "Me neither. But it could happen. It could happen to any girl, any day."

"Why'd you keep me?" The photo lay next to the cigarette case, which lay next to her locket, which lay next to a red rose in a crack pipe vase. It stared at us, an origami elephant. Its real origins were never explained.

"Never really thought about it. The money was good

and things have a way of working themselves out. You put your worries at the back of your mind and fate handles it. Did you know Hugh Hefner owns the Y in Hollywood?"

People shouldn't talk when they're dying, even if it takes a week longer than anticipated. The rose and cigarettes had outlasted her.

Fooled by a photo she'd supposedly taken in her year of freedom roaming the beds and couches of Tinsel Town. It was her accent, they'd all told her. They couldn't hammer the hilljack out of her voice. She'd accepted her fate and pointed her bloated stomach back towards the Appalachian Mountains. My dad was anyone and everyone - an aged Richard Burton or an up-and-coming Brad Pitt.

It was a fairly modest story, as far as tall tales go – and perfectly reasonable to a child.

Moral of the story: nineteen year olds shouldn't dream.

My legacy is under my arms and head, and behind my elevated legs. Blue shag carpeting above a graveyard of failed auditions, gold-framed photos and celebrity names for their lauded memories.

To burn the trailer to the ground or shrine it. To unpack my bags in her crimson bedroom or put out my thumb as she did. To buy pre-natal vitamins or call planned parenthood.

The twist: Patrick is the name of every boy in every story, the boy that's nice but overlooked, whose shoulder is always waiting. But Patricks are sly – they never sleep on the couch after the drive home from the wake. They stop at the county liquor store for a bottle of Jack and wait for you to invite them into your cold mother's room.

Buried in a Roberto Cavalli knock-off, hair like Marilyn Monroe. The wig obscured the damage the bullet did to the back of her left ear.

I told Patrick about running away, about her ultimate dissatisfaction with every dog. So eager and gorgeous, so interchangeable. Little doppelgängers of Celeste. We dragged suitcases of heels from underneath her bed to laugh at their audacity. Stilettos, in this mud. Suede, to wear in a diner.

Some were dusty.

"Haven't you ever wanted to reach through the mirror and strangle your own reflection?" I'd asked. He didn't understand or care. But he had sealed my mother's lips for good. His clothes didn't stink of formaldehyde, details like that are celluloid dreams.

Patrick will call, in – a glance at my watch; my arm is lead – approximately nineteen minutes.

Open bags or matches. Truth or lie.

Hollywood or Vegas, they're both the same from matted carpet on a singlewide's floor.

A dark spot on the baseboard catches my eye and I hitch – laugh or a croak, it's hard to say. This is where she intended her outline be drawn.

Celeste's locket falls, resting just to the left of my collarbone, a glittery ten karat noose.

'To Thine Own Self Be True' it reads. I mean, of course it does.

Gold is a lie.

I stare at Jack Lallane's portrait, cocked head, glittering eyes, short attention span. "Gold is a lie." His collar sparkles.

From the kitchen, the robin's egg blue phone trills the future and the past into the present. The timing is off.

The photo crunches like tiny bones in my fist.

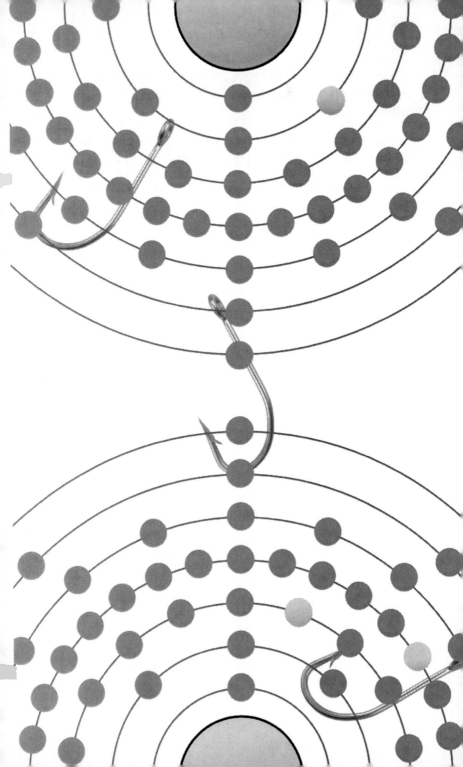

TROTLINES

Worst thing about tuna from the can was the sound the fork made running along the edge – Ruby gritted her teeth and flashed back to a kindergarten she barely remembered, when the boards were black and chalk dust floated in the shafts of light. She couldn't imagine what little kids would stare at now, with their squeaky marker boards.

Kids don't stare at nothin' now, just through, she corrected herself, and balanced the empty can on a tower of other empty cans. Somewhere beneath the mess was the trash bucket, but she had an agreement with the twins not to burn trash when they were gone.

No matter how long it took for one of them to remember to haul it out back. Apocalypse or not, the place was still a damned home, not a hog pen. There was a lighter shaped like a woman in a bikini, she snatched it on her way out the door.

"Ruby!"

Goddamned Nazi teenagers.

"What?" Screen door slamming behind her, she lit a stale Marlboro, twisting her hair up off her neck and curling her toes in the grass. First nice day in a week at least, fuck the boys. She wasn't spending another minute on the couch watching the only station left – it was broadcasted di-rect from Teddy's basement. Just an old man finally tired of shooting shit, going progressively insane.

"You better go back in. It's dangerous." Naked to the waist of his jeans, a tanned nineteen year old hooked his thumbs in his belt loops and squinted like Josey Wales. For punctuation, he spit.

"The fuck it is," Ruby skipped to the picnic table and flashed her legs at him, crossing and uncrossing them, toenails redder than her hair.

Silver glimmered here and there in the tall grass at the edge of the yard, a thousand empties that would never announce a married couple's farewell to solitude. Mike and Grig set up a perimeter of alarms with the sophistication of the Frog Brothers. Most all their survival methods were at this intelligence level, but stiffs weren't all that swift. Maybe bloodsuckers were smart, but braineaters didn't have the sense to step over a cluster of cans or around a deep hole.

"I ain't seen a corpse so much as twitch in a week. I wanna lay in the sun." Untying the bottom of her halter, she let it hang, no hint of a breeze to help the show. "Where's your brother?"

"Bev's dogs was barkin' half the night, we been up at her place checkin'."

"She all right?"

"Roberta had six pups. Bev cussed us for wakin' her up after she'd been up with the dogs, but then she made biscuits and gravy."

"She did not! Why didn't you come get me?"

Mike's teeth were white as any Colgate ad. "Come on, Ruby. George got ate first night, and Bev's pushin' fifty. If we'd hauled Miss Perky Tits up the holler with us there would'na been no biscuits and gravy."

"You're a charmer, Mike Forshey, really you are. If Grig's up there givin' it to Bev he can sleep somewhere else."

Mike giggled. "Maybe he will. You don't cook like Bev."

"What about you?" Ruby dragged the halter over her head with a yank that undid her hair as well.

"Cookin' ain't all there is to love." He laid his rifle across his shoulders and hooked a hand over each end like he was in the stocks. "Any point in me comin' in, or you just teasin' ?"

Shrugging, she dragged on her cigarette. "Just teasin'. Too hot for it."

Nodding, Mike sighed. "We found us some jumpsuits in the doc's back room, I told Grig we oughta drag off as many as we can before August and they really take to stinkin'. Anyway, we'll get the air conditioner workin' tomorrow."

The twins were built for this. Hell, most she knew - used to know- were built for it. If there'd been alarms, if the highway'd run through the town, if it'd happened in the day, Coalton would probably still be pretty much the same.

Prime attack time in a one stoplight town is just before dawn on a Sunday morning. Everybody is passed the fuck out, and the walls will be painted with brains and guts before anyone gets the satellite tuned to the national news that said to lock the damned doors and remain calm.

Half were dead before the church bell rang. Ruby's dad had bit her mama in the throat and Ruby brained him with her little brother's aluminum tee ball bat before she thought about it. With Mama locked in one bedroom and Tommy in another, Ruby sat in the morning light in her panties and Lady Gaga shirt chainsmoking Daddy's menthols and listened to gunshots and screams in the rest of Wallwork Estates Trailer Court. She didn't turn the light on, didn't look out the door. By the time the cellophane crunched empty in her fist, the noise had died down, and Daddy had started to move.

First thing, she'd looked at her hands, and smelled the empty pack. She watched Daddy twitch on the yellow kitchen floor and tore it open, looking for powder residue, hoping for something to help her believe she was fucked up, that it was all in her head. Nothing.

Mama'd started thumping on the door. Still, Ruby was sure it was meth, or maybe coke cut with something weird. She passed her room where Mama thump thump thumped and Tommy's door where there was no sound and kicked open the composite board door of her parents' bedroom. Knee-walking across the waterbed, she knocked down roach clips, hemos and a wedding photo before discovering the Ruger's clip under Tommy's last report card. The gun was in the nightstand, the clip was hid. Daddy heard about gun safety, he wasn't stupid.

Ruby hadn't felt her hand on the gun, but the clip slid home like a slick cock, and she ran down the hall, past the thump thump thump, pistol at her shoulder like on the cop shows.

Floating. She'd heard her feet skitter onto the linoleum. Standing over her old man, facedown in his factory blues with blood in his hair, Ruby whispered "I'm sorry." But when he rolled over and looked up with eyes as milky as poor old Roberta with her cataracts, the scream that came out tore her throat. She screamed and screamed, and the last she knew of her dad was his long arm snatching for her ankle. Ruby emptied the clip in his wide open mouth.

The sound of the gun dry-firing over and over in her hands was like a clock, soothing her down off a ledge, and when Ruby realized she was no longer screaming, she also realized there were two men in the living room.

"Ruby Mullins," one twin had said (this was before she'd had over four weeks to learn to tell them apart). "Didn't know you had it in you."

They never blamed her for pointing the gun at them both, click, click, click, click.

"You gotta wash your legs," the other one said, then matter-of-factly pushed the bedroom doors open, firing off a few shots in each.

Since that month had passed, she was glad she never knew which one killed her mom and Tommy.

"Whatcha thinkin' 'bout, Red?"

Blinking up into the sun and back to the picnic table, she answered "Tommy."

Mike crossed to her in a few long steps. If it had been a different place, a different life, he might've cupped her face in his hands and kissed her, telling her it would be okay, and reminded her about the good things – the stiffs seemed pretty well killed off, her family was in heaven, the garden was coming up good, and Mike Henderson's cow had a late calf. Maybe even added some flattery - she was still seventeen and still beautiful, and he and Grig hadn't noticed the black roots in her red hair or that her carpet didn't match her drapes. That sooner or later everything would seem kind of normal.

Instead, he spit and said "Grig ain't fuckin' Bev. He's workin' on her tractor. He's fixin' to trade her for a pup. He wants you to have a pup, Ruby."

She laughed and kissed him on the mouth. He felt her boob out of instinct, but it was okay. The miracle really wasn't that she had survived a wave of the Apocalypse or whatever, but that she had slept between twins in a queen-sized bed for this long and wasn't pregnant.

"I'm goin'," Mike groaned, as she pushed him away. She lit another cigarette. "We're gonna hunt a little this evenin', and day after tomorrow we're goin' back out to the highway with Henderson to check out the rest of the trucks. If we ain't seen nothin' by then you can go with us, okay? If we ain't seen nothin'."

Ruby spread her top on the table and lay back, the fabric shielding her shoulderblades from scraping. "Okay. Have fun. And if the pups look like Roberta see if she's got one with differn't color eyes."

"Picky bitch."

She closed her eyes, hearing the grass rustle against his legs. "What's for supper?" He called back.

"Pie!" Ruby yelled, and his laughter followed him.

In fifteen minutes she was bored and sweaty.

In twenty the back of her brain was itching.

In thirty she knew she'd been lied to, and went to find her boots.

Ruby hadn't been scared since she shot her Daddy in the face – as far as worst case scenarios, that was it, so what was there to fear? She picked her way along the crick in the brush, looking for the flash of hooks. If she found the twins' trotlines, she was close to the cabin. Wasn't long before the pistol was heavy in her belt and she didn't care what they were doing anymore - foraging was exciting. She'd been sittin' on her ass too long.

A good-sized trout flipped in the sun, splashing water, and Ruby stopped to push the line down underwater so it could breathe. Didn't like this type of fishing, but it saved time. If they caught a couple more she could fry 'em up on the grill, and dig proper in the cellar of their house's former resident for something to go with it. Corn on the cob was all she really wanted but -

Ruby saw the cabin and heard the stiff call in the same instant. She ran, pistol in hand, thorns pulling red lines in her legs. Pressing her face to the door, she listened.

Laughter.

"Motherfuckers!" Ruby yelled, and under her angry shoulder the door gave. She fell onto the dirt at the feet of a tied girl wearing a pink high heel. A dead, tied girl wearing a pink high heel.

The stiff howled; Ruby stared up at it. Grig and Mike were frozen in a cloud of pot smoke, their jaws gaping like the stiff's.

Pushing herself to her feet, Ruby felt her throat close. "You fuckin' pervs," she whispered, and looked around. The plank table held the collected contents of what would soon be all they needed to cook meth, if they could find the ingredients. Cold medicine was the one thing hard to come by these days. Weed in a pile around a purple water bong on the chipped coffee table in front of them, they were both fully dressed.

The stiff was not. She was greenish grey all over and dripped white at the mouth, her shoulder bone completely exposed. Her nipples had gone black, and her lips, and all she had on besides the shoe was a pair of stained white granny panties. Barbed wire looped around her neck, staple-gunned to the back wall under each of her ears. Her waist was pinned the same. Its, Ruby reminded herself. Its waist. The girl thing howled, eyes white.

"Ruby, we didn't -"

She trained her gun on Grig, even though the protest was Mike's. "You boys been fuckin' that thing?"

His eyes were red, but his mouth made a straight line. He folded his arms and leaned back into the dirty cushion. Quietly, "No. But we been thinkin' on it 'bout three days now."

"Dammit, Grig -"

"Shut the fuck up, Mike." Ruby kicked the plank table and smashed all the cookware as it landed. "This is what you two been doin'? Bev ain't got no pups, Henderson ain't got no calf, and there ain't nothin' left in the factory, is there?"

Grig shook his head. "Bev's got pups. But yeah, mainly we been sittin' up here wonderin' what to do with Sarah."

Ruby swung the gun, and with a loud crack Sarah Stiff's head jerked, then she dangled in the wire.

Mike put his head in his hands.

"So this is what it's gonna be like?" Ruby asked, and

cocked her head. The pistol dangled at her thigh.

"Who the fuck knows?" Grig shoved weed into the bowl and reached for the lighter. "I'm bored. Mike's bored. Ever'body's bored. This End of the World is the most boring shit that ever happened. We gotta figure out what the fuck to do, forever." He lit the bong and took a long hit, coughing.

"We had to do that anyway, dipshit," Ruby answered, but there was no fight in her. Hell, there was no fight left in Ted, even, broadcasting from his compound in the desert.

"Don't you ever wish you'd been rescued by someone you woulda talked to in high school?" Mike asked.

As she stepped over the coffee table, they each offered Ruby, last fall's Coal Festival Queen, a hand. She fell between them on the futon. "No," she answered, and didn't think it over, because the truth didn't matter. Grig passed her the bong, and she laid her head against his shoulder.

"Promise you didn't fuck it?"

"Swear on Mom's grave. Mike didn't neither. We was just curious."

Ruby hit the bong, coughed heartily, and handed it to Mike. Her head switched to his shoulder, rotating between them from habit. "You think Sarah was prettier than me – before she was dead, I mean?"

"Fuck no," the twins answered in stereo.

Eventually they laid the futon flat, and didn't leave the cabin until all three of them were sweaty and tired. On the walk back they smacked at mosquitos, and a few lightning bugs blinked to each other.

On the trotline, the trout flipped and splashed, but Ruby forgot all about it.

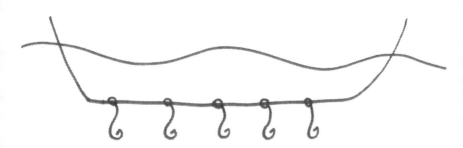

Draw the fish you caught!

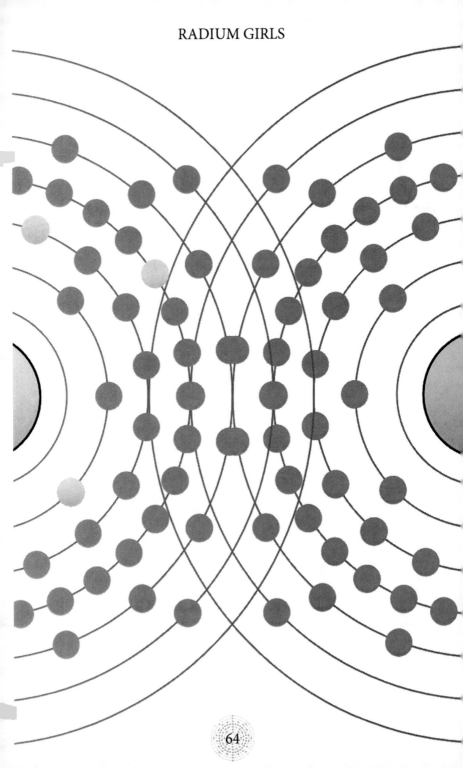

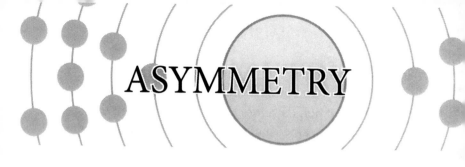

ASYMMETRY

By sixteen she could no longer remember a time when she knew which was her mother. Neither answered to Mother; neither answered much of anything she said.

Her first memories were of the picture books in her blue bedroom.

The shelves were lined with toys – two music boxes with broken gears, their identical ballerinas frozen in identical icy poses. A wind-up seesaw missing its key, stopped even, balanced, a faceless girl at each end. Porcelain dolls, temples touching, eyes shining and secretive. But in the books there were drawings of men and women, a child between them. Her four-year-old self traced the men's faces with curious hands. She had never seen a Him. The princesses in the towers waited for Him, the devil that spun straw into gold was Him, the man in the sky that burned the bad people was Him.

Did you make me? she'd asked.

The twins' eyes met.

Not together, one answered.

But you're ours all the same, said the other.

In one of them she had grown and swam, a single mermaid in a single bowl, but she could not guess which.

At six she spent most of her time on the porch swing, the wind chime's rusty metal efforts the closest thing to a lullaby she heard. It clinked and shimmered desperately, aching to soothe her as she lay with a teddy bear under each arm and thanked it quietly. There was no other half of her, therefore she was alone. From the vegetable garden came laughter and gibberish, a language not her own and a language they did not teach her. They taught her the 'outside language' and how to read from sepia books, flanking her at the kitchen table.

I know there are schools, she'd said.

Out there is not for us, one answered.

Out there they're not like us, said the other.

But I am not like you, she didn't say. I am not part of this Us.

She realized they hadn't meant her inclusion, anyway. There was no word for Mother in their language, she supposed, but hundreds and hundreds for We.

So the wind chime was her mother's voice, the moon her mother's face. The wind chime asked in broken notes, the moon tilted its head, waiting for answers. Nighttime conversations of whispers floated in and out her open window while her chin rested on the sill.

At the edge of the driveway she stood for hours, eight years old, to study the outside faces glimpsed in occasional cars. She searched for doubles through the gravel dust, and her surprise was never exhausted by the absence. I am one of Them, she thought. Pairs of yellow butterflies danced in rising circles in the light fluttering between the branches of the big tree, taunting her. Beneath it, all things were halves of a whole.

Where is mine? she'd asked.

In the mirror, said one.

In the mirror you're never incomplete, said the other.

Their eyes locked in pity at the loneliness they could not understand.

Twelve and wild with emptiness, she'd run on bare feet and brown legs through the fields, forever and ever, tall grass whipping her skin, sunshine filling her lungs -- and heart. It swelled and broke with every breath, cracking over and over with the double beat in her chest. In a clearing squatted a wide and gnarled stump, day after day she found herself upon it, reaching for the sky, spreading her fingers with face upturned, becoming the other half of this tree. Sun between her fingers, sun leaking from her eyes, she dreamed of the roots spread beneath the ground in a mirror image.

She ran out of questions, forgot her voice. She was the animal that roamed the grounds of their castle – a skittish deer they watched with curious eyes, but never extended a hand to tame.

The mirror in her room was the only mirror in the house, and she saw it for what it was: a surrogate, a stand-in, the only thing they knew to give her to help bear what she lacked. She smashed it into hundreds of miniature sixteen year old girls – the temptation to count them seized her, sure the number of shards would be even, casting her out once again.

The stairs moaned at the twins' rapid ascent, two faces, two pairs of wide dark eyes in her doorway.

You've killed her, said one.

What will you do now? asked the other.

I could leave, she said.

Silence clung to the corners of the room.

It's time to let her go, said one.

And the other said nothing. A pale arm extended, and with a ragged fingernail scratched at the skull of one of the dolls on the seesaw, breaking the balance, revealing a sliver of blond beneath the hand-painted hair.

That night in the dark house, her window stood open and the moonlight tossed a gossamer rectangle across the shards of glass. She pushed the pieces carefully around.

Outside, the wind chime shivered silver notes, silver tears, and downstairs one twin cried.

Which of these girls is not like the others?

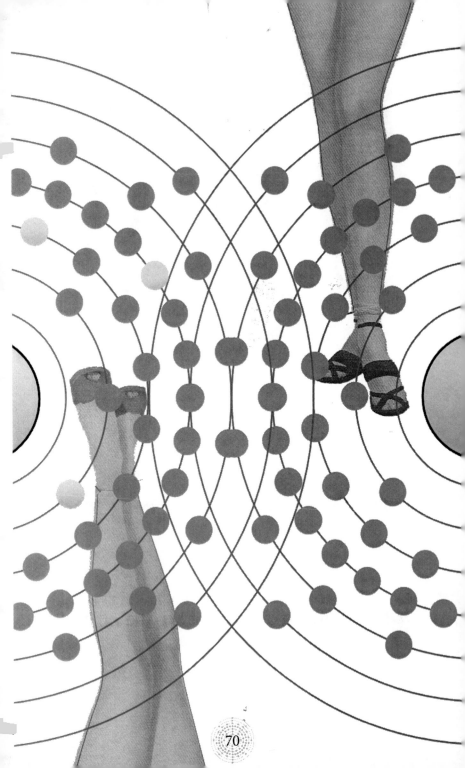

A Brief Conversation
While Buying a Drink in Checkers Lounge,
Eight Years Coming

INT. DIVE BAR - EVENING

We're in a mostly empty bar and when I
say we I mean ME. The only options for
entertainment are avoiding eye contact
with two creepy guys playing pool or
continuing a conversation with a FRIEND
long forgotten.

>   WHAT I ASKED
>   You remember Jimmy's
>   wife?

>   WHAT HE ANSWERED
>   Her name was Jenny. She
>   a was 6'2" blonde with
>   classic Irish features
>   and a monstrous rack who
>   raped me while on acid
>   and a host of other cheap
>   shit including a bottle
>   of Aftershock when I was
>   fourteen. I remember the
>   ceiling being a lot of
>   colors.

>   WHAT I SAID
>   Ha. I didn't - I thought
>   I saw you over there, I
>   never knew what was up
>   with her.   (Cont.)

WHAT I SAID (Cont.)
But I remember that cheap
shit, and I remember, she
had one of those touch
lamps with the gold base
and the frosted flower
shade so if you tap tap
tapped it the ceiling
turned into Lazer Floyd,
but the trip was never
good, she just sold it to
get the boys to come over
when Jimmy was in for
manufacturing.

WHAT HE SAID
I don't remember you.

WHAT I DIDN'T SAY
I never met you, but I knew who
you were. Weekends I mostly
spent two trailers down, my
best friend was Jenny's niece
Heaven Lee. We seen some of you
and the other boys go in and
out, and HL said she talked to
you all the time when I wasn't
there but she was full of shit.
You guys were older, me and HL
were twelve that summer Jimmy
was inside. Jenny'd pay us a
bottle of Boone's if we'd watch
the baby when she had company,
and HL showed me the trick of

putting NyQuil on the binky and
BOOM Jimmy Jr. was out for the
night and we'd sit on the steps
and smoke the last hits off her
mom's cigarette butts we dug
out of the ashtray, listen to the
noise coming out of Jenny's and
sort of pretend we were there,
like the light coming out her
windows just about reached HL's
driveway and we could hear the
music even if we couldn't tell
what it was.

HL's mom was gone every
Saturday night back then, and
we'd give the baby a bottle and
some knock+out drops and spend
the last hour of daylight in the
bathroom with HL's big purple
case full of dime store make+
up, then plant ourselves on
the steps like it was nothin',
waiting for someone to notice
what big girls we were and what
big eyes we had, what big mouths
we had and maybe offer us a
whole cigarette or a real beer,
but it never happened. You and
Max were over at the same time
a lot, I remember Jenny yelling
you out the front door and Max
staying in most nights, me and
HL holding our breath, and

even though her mom's fucking
dream catcher wind chime rang
like a fire alarm most nights
you never looked. You'd smoke
cigarettes in the yard and bust
bottles off that bathtub Mary
in the lot in between, get the
old woman in the blue trailer's
Pomeranian going, but you never
looked up at us, not once.

We never had a chance. Never
more than a half hour before
Max'd laugh and kick the door
open and you'd cuss your way
back inside, and Jenny'd block
the light from the whole doorway
when she latched the screen, and
you can bet your ass she knew
we were out there. HL always
said the same bullshit thing,
too, when you went back inside
+ ⎕Fuckin' pussy,⎕ but she
wouldn't say shit either. I had
no tits and she needed braces,
we had nothing to offer a boy
old as you + we thought you
were highschool, at least.

It was the last weekend in July,
the last time we saw you was,
and the baby was out cold and
Max had stopped coming over.
Jenny had her hair all folded

up in foil doin' her roots and
said Jimmy was getting out in
two weeks, and she let us in on
the celebration by giving us two
hits of that rat poison shit and
not making us leave. She rinsed
her hair in the sink and shared
her menthols, laughing at us
sorta I think, but we didn't
care. I tapped that goddamned
lamp for what seemed like a
week, taptaptap, tap, tap, tap,
taptaptap, over and over, HL
laughing on the green carpet,
grass growing up around her
wrists and forehead, and we
were Grown Up‡

Then you knocked on the door
and Jenny told us to get the
fuck out.

You didn't even look at us as
we passed, but I was walking
on marshmallows and couldn't
remember where we'd left the
baby, so the night was busy
while we hunted the yards
and the shrubs and peeked in
windows and HL lost a flip‡
flop, and we crossed lot to lot
like it was a checkerboard,
only going diagonal, ringing
wind chimes and studying fat

porcelain frogs in flowerbeds
looking everywhere for that
goddamned baby, even behind the
Bathtub Mary, Full of Grace and
Christmas Lights, and the dew
was burning off before we came
down, bone tired and thirsty,
and heard the baby crying from
Jenny's because of course he'd
been there all night, all along,
and HL's mom's pickup was
in the driveway already and
there was a tiny, exciting and
horrible moment we thought we
might be In Trouble before we
limped inside and remembered it
didn't matter.

HL's mom was passed out on the
couch, and HL was pouring two
cups full of black cherry Kool+
aid when we heard a car honk +
I saw you, out the window over
the sink, get in your brother's
car + an old Crown Vic + but
it was just the back of your
head and one shoulder of
your jacket, the first and last
Sunday morning I ever saw you.

By the following weekend Jimmy
was home, a week early, and
Jenny had two black eyes and
everything went back to normal

and changed all at once, if
that makes sense + by the end
of the summer Heaven's mom
got married and they moved
out of the trailer court, a few
weeks before Jenny's place
burned down, burned inside out
and Jimmy went back in for
manufacturing.

We got to highschool two years
later you were still there, so
you were either a lot younger
or a lot stupider than we
thought, but wore the same
jacket + and Heaven had her
braces off and still wouldn't
talk to you.

Jenny and Jimmy's baby started
second grade with my little
brother this fall, and I swear
to god if I could've thought
of one other thing to say, to
finally say, I would have.

WHAT I DID SAY
I just wanted to ask you
something, anything,
that the answer'd be
Yes.

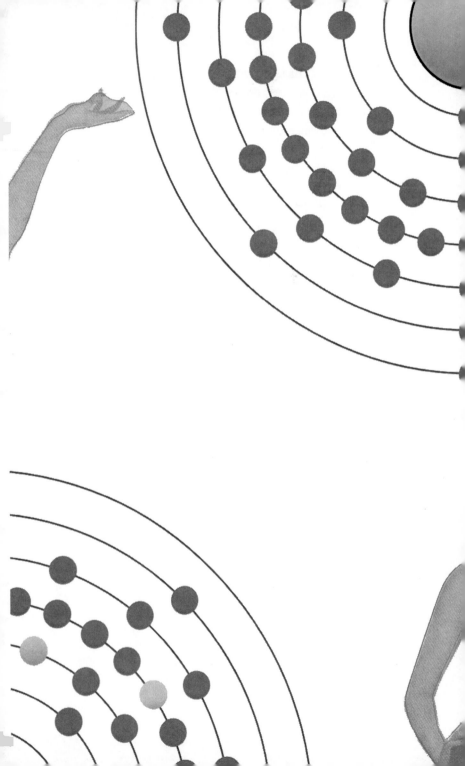

SHORT TENDON

More Human opened two shops down from Hammer & Nails in the last strip mall existing in Evans Collective – maybe the last strip mall anywhere.

Marsla asked Grandmere, More human than what?

Grandmere sighed and spun her chair away, electing instead to lighten the mood with a song her grandmother used to play. Marsla laughed at the parallel lyrics and rhyming.

Twyla, Marsla's genetic identical, did not laugh. As an employee of Hammer & Nails, she wanted to know why a modification franchise would open in a collective as small and remote as theirs in the first place. In just one week their business had diminished, as teens elected to have their fingertips replaced and their nails metalled instead of just gilded or magnetized. Suddenly all the salons were ancient, un-hip.

Grandmere tried to explain that if the fringes could be won over, anyone could. Twyla didn't care. She said she wished she were Asian so she could work at More Human, which had sprung up overnight with its own staff.

Where did you learn that word?

What word?

Asian.

Twyla laughed and said it was what the old women told her the employees at the new place were – they all had god-hair of black, almond eyes and flat cheekbones.

Grandmere covered her eyes with gnarled hands, pursing her lips in disgust. It's a trick, she explained. Are the heads real?

Neither girl had entertained the possibility that they were not.

The optometrists were hit hardest, fastest. Their expansion of eye color selection did nothing to compete with eye replacement, and a trend appeared in the area – Husky eyes, though no one was sure what it meant – of one blue eye and one brown. No one scheduled corrective surgery anymore. The two optometrists folded up quietly and disappeared within the month.

The salons hung on longer, with the return of god-colors and faster machines - and lower prices. Purple, silver, gold and blue hair gave way to 'blond,' 'strawberry blond' and 'auburn.' Women compared their flesh-toned scalp stitches and raved about the painlessness of the Switch and Stitch machine.

I thought the modification centers made metal parts, Marsla said. Everyone in the ads have silver parts.

Wait, Grandmere said. She looked at her arthritic hands. First they blend in – then they stand out.

Twyla rolled her eyes and flipped her blond hair. She pointed a metal fingernail and accused Grandmere of being a cloud of doom.

In three months, Hammer & Nails was gone, and the two remaining salons were for sale – machines included. New ads appeared on the More Human mail tablets - appendage adjustment, augmentation, improvement.

Slender flesh-toned hands, plump fish lips, small and feminine feet, straight noses.

Still no silver.

One afternoon Marsla returned from tutoring to find Grandmere staring at the wall, at the huge projection of perfect hands in the More Human ad. Her head was tilted, purple hair in a fancy updo. Thinking her asleep, Marsla tiptoed past.

I've made an appointment for Friday, Grandmere announced without turning. Do you remember the piano in Mr. Chronon's Museum? I played one once. I would like to learn, and I believe Mr. Chronon could teach me.

She didn't remember what a piano was, but Marsla kept quiet.

Friday evening, Marsla and Twyla sat on the floor pillows, mirror images except for their hair, awaiting her return.

They both stiffened at the laughter at the door, but before either could rise to assist, light glinted off a shiny silver hand on the entrance buttons, and behind it came Grandmere's sleeve, then Grandmere's smiling face, and Mr. Chronon.

Purple hair loose to the waist, Grandmere chatted briefly at the entrance with the older gentleman. The girls heard *Tomorrow night, yes, lovely*, then the shuffle of receding footsteps.

Why hide what is obviously new? She waved her new hands in the air, snapped her fingers. I will not disguise them. They are beautiful.

Grandmere knitted the night away. At the kitchen

table next morning she wrote in a language Marsla had never seen before - writing at all was uncommon. Cursive, Grandmere said. She wore her clothes from the night before. On the table was a finished scarf and real sheets of paper, covered with sketches of faces and hands.

Another month passed. More Human expanded, buying up the entire strip mall and hiring on most of the former salons' employees to perform superficial procedures and preserving the original staff for modifications. But no one used that word - 'modification.' The collective's inhabitant's shimmered in the evening sunrise. Light glinted off their self-improvements. Marsla passed Mr. Chronon 'jogging' – cane discarded, silver calves above his white sneakers. Twyla was hired and all her earnings poured back into a 50/50 fund the company provided for self-improvement. Twyla wanted new cheekbones, flat ones, and her eyes tilted. A transparent agenda: she thought the more Asian-looking, the more chance for advancement within the company.

Six months after opening, half the town was employed by More Human and the rest had been touched by them in some way. Agriculturalists received stipends for allowing the corporation's designers to study the horses, cows; to watch the agriculturalists themselves as they moved, the muscle groups used, the repetitive labors.

Feeding the Percherons, Marsla was discovered by a designer. He wore white coveralls and studied her, recorder on, for some moments without speaking.

You are like these animals, calm, confident, he said finally. Would you have their eyes?

Her laugh surprised him, he lifted his eyebrows. Do you know what a Husky is?

At the shake of her head he tapped buttons on his tablet. This is a dog, he told her. The breed of this one is a Husky.

Morning dusk fell as they explored his notes and pictures. Marsla saw flamingos and fish and more dogs, and something called a cat.

This is the next big thing in eyes, he confided. Just wait until next year. He sighed at her lack of excitement. Just go in and see. At least see the surgeon about your finger.

Her finger. The UV streetlights led her home, and she flexed her hand repeatedly, unable to straighten her pinky. She'd never been able.

It's just a little funky, Grandmere had told her.

What's funky? she'd asked.

Morbid curiosity finally collided with a legitimate excuse.

Silver was scarce, tasteful. A demure girl in a white coat led Marsla through the salon area, buzzing with customers. Twyla winked in her direction from the control pad of a multi-colorizer, and Marsla noticed her brand new blue and brown eyes.

Dr. Chanel Ping, a white nameplate on the steel door read, and the girl knocked once before pressing it open.

Lovely to meet you. A Nubian hand extended to meet hers across a wide glass desk with nothing on it. Marsla took it, eyes following the arm to the shoulder and across. Where the other girls buttoned their coats to the throat, Dr. Ping's hung open, and Marsla saw the shiny purple stitching join dark flesh and light just above the collarbone. Her face and head were remarkably like the

other girls'. She gestured Marsla into the chair opposite. I
know what you're thinking, she smiled. And yes, this is my
real head. The skin, no, the face, no, but I assure you this is
my skull and brain et cetera, et cetera, she circled her hands
in the air before steepling her brown fingers.

Marsla said nothing.

Your gemini works here, doesn't she? Dr. Ping
asked. Without waiting for an answer she continued, It's
interesting to see the… before and after, if you know what I
mean. You're untouched, aren't you? That's even your God-
hair – oh, don't blush, I'm an expert, of course I can tell the
difference between god-hair and God-hair. Dr. Ping twisted
her fingers at her lips. Your secret is safe with me. Now, let's
see your hand.

The walk home was tricky, looking the whole time
at her finger. A short tendon, Dr. Ping had explained. She
explained corrective surgery and hospital alternatives,
then brought out a tray of 'alternate' fingers in all shades
and colors, outlining the removal of the old at the bottom
knuckle and placement of the new, and of the tiny, tiny cost
of such a thing as a finger. Marsla was fingerprinting the
tablet of consent and the white light buzzed over her hand
while she relaxed on a pink plastic chair, then here she was
– taking the long way as the light glinted off the silver. As
Grandmere had said, Why hide what is obviously new?

Marsla hesitated at Museum Drive, but one of Mr.
Chronon's windows was open, and Grandmere's laughter
accompanied by a careful tune met her across the field. She
heard clapping, and imagined Mr. Chronon standing next
to her unaided. Marsla finally remembered what the piano
looked like – and what Grandmere's silver hands must
look like walking across those black and white rectangles.

Smiling, Marsla went on. She hummed the tune Grandmere was making, and flexed her hand. She would show the designer tomorrow. His eyes had been the same color, his hair a common blue.

A year passed.

Yelling downstairs, again. Twyla couldn't make the payment on her permanent Husky eyes – the first set had been temporaries, to test out compatibility, buyer satisfaction, it was all in the tabletwork. To make matters worse, she was done with Husky eyes. Didn't Grandmere understand that Calico eyes would be available in three months?

Grandmere was in default on her hand repair loan, only Twyla didn't know. It had been a cloudy midnight Marsla had crept downstairs to hear her crying on the phone. Unusual wear – such as piano lessons, knitting, typing – were not covered. Mr. Chronon was experiencing the same problem – jogging, hiking, swimming – with his knees and legs. Both of them had sold large chunks of property for repairs, but it wasn't enough....

You're late for work! Marsla yelled down the stairs. Fuck you and your cat eyes!

Where did you learn the word Fuck? Grandmere asked.

What's a cat? Twyla asked.

Both questions went unanswered, and Marsla dragged herself back to the toilette to be sick.

The designers were gone, along with their stipends and studies. For Marsla, one was still sort of here.

He no longer answered her tablets.

The collectivesfolk were literally falling apart. More Human hadn't expanded in size or staff, but deliveries of 'permanent' parts arrived daily. Women gathered in hushed groups in market corners, one in sunglasses, another in gloves, a third's invisible misery only evident by her tears. Canes and wheelchairs reappeared. Scarves cropped up. The hospital was understaffed for the emergency surgeries and began taking interns off the street. Girls once working at More Human to pay for cosmetic adjustments now worked at the hospital to pay off surgery. The town divided, those backing into themselves and those desperate to move forward. The open slots at More Human filled as soon as they opened, and Twyla flipped her black bob shamelessly, replacing fingertips and running the Switch and Stitch machine with a demure smile and itchy eyes.

Someone will break, Grandmere said.

Marsla opened her mouth to answer that everyone already had, but changed her mind.

Take me to see Mr. Chronon, Marsla, Grandmere whispered. I want you to hear me play, while I still can.

The museum isn't everything the world used to be, Mr. Chronon explained, their footsteps echoing on the wooden floor and amplifying the tap of his cane, It's just everything I want to remember about the world.

Bicycle, automobile, broom, hair dryer, paperback, guitar, dreidel, kerosene lamp, crayons, mailbox... on and on he rambled, some of these things attaching to images in Marsla's mind.

He turned a goldish-colored round attachment and pushed open a door at the end of the hall. Inside was a– a-

This is a Grand Piano, Marsla, Mr. Chronon rattled

off details, his eyes never leaving Grandmere as she seated herself on the bench and pushed back the cover of the black and white rectangles.

Light poured in the glass and turned the wood floor a color Marsla had never seen. Slowly, Mr. Chronon walked window to window, pushing them up. Grandmere's eyes followed his laboured progress.

These are folding chairs, he said, and offered one to Marsla. Next to her and off from Grandmere, his eyes were wet as she flexed her metal fingers.

Oil can, oil can, Grandmere croaked, laughing with Mr. Chronon, the joke lost to Marsla.

One more concert?

Grandmere nodded. One more.

Keys, that's what they were called. Keys.

The silver hands fell over the keys, attacking them, wooing them, coaxing, and the sound was like nothing Marsla had ever heard. It lived on its own, in the air, in the light, in her blood. Tears glowed on the cheeks of Grandmere and Mr. Chronon, and the music lived in the tears, too.

Inside, Marsla felt a shift, and placed a hand on her belly. Beneath her palm came another bubble, another turn – What is this? she whispered.

Beethoven, Mr. Chronon whispered back.

More Human burned that night. No one protested, no one tried to stop it. Little by little the residents of Evans Collective gathered in the parking lot and formed a loose circle to watch.

There was a quiet satisfaction in the smoke, the orange aura, the metal curling and turning black. By morning there was only the stink and embers. Most of the crowd dissolved and drifted off to their private pains, Twyla knuckling her sensitive orbs from smoke and tears.

A few hung around, poking at the ashes, searching for nothing.

Marsla was among them. Hands in her loose jacket's pockets, she kicked at the place the front door had been.

The moonlight threw two bent and crooked shadows near her and she watched without turning. They tilted their heads, becoming a united absence of light, and with difficulty twined their shadow hands.

She took the long way home, past the closed windows and the dead piano. Marsla whispered that magic word: *Beethoven*.

Which animal's eyes would YOU choose?

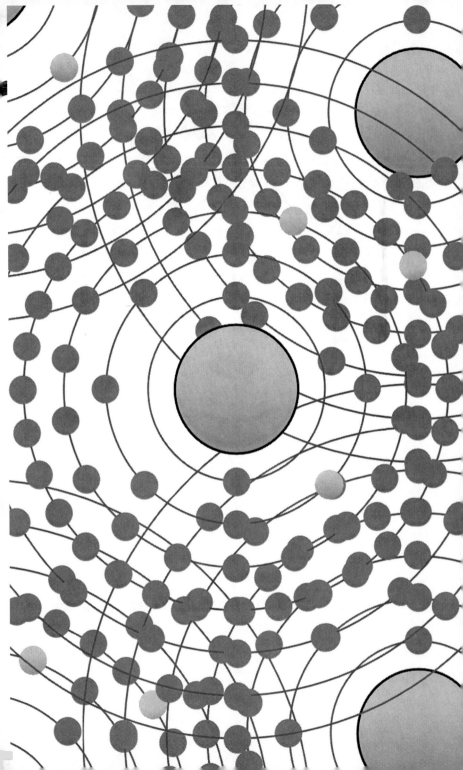

THE OLD UNIVERSE

A sheet of typing paper reading 'MARS' hung
above the kitchen doorway.

She said I didn't answer but the screen was
unlocked, I was painting and didn't look up.

"I knew you'd come today." In the photo she took
I wore red devil horns.

She washed the dishes and I asked her to leave,
but it was nothing personal. There had been a
Night Before and would be another - I needed a
nap in between.

It was a cowardly way, I tell her today, of
waiting to die. If the roof hadn't weakened and
caved under the rain, I would've not waken. If
the roof hadn't literally fallen in, I would've
died.

You were already dead, she answers. There was
nothing left of you.

I don't remember any of this, I say (but maybe I
do - she didn't mention the horns).

The Jesus clock collage and all the long socks
were lost in the flood, the purple figure
painting and notebooks full of lurid details
- smeared and blurry, lines bled together -
chicken scratch memories obliterated.

I burned them. Should have told her.

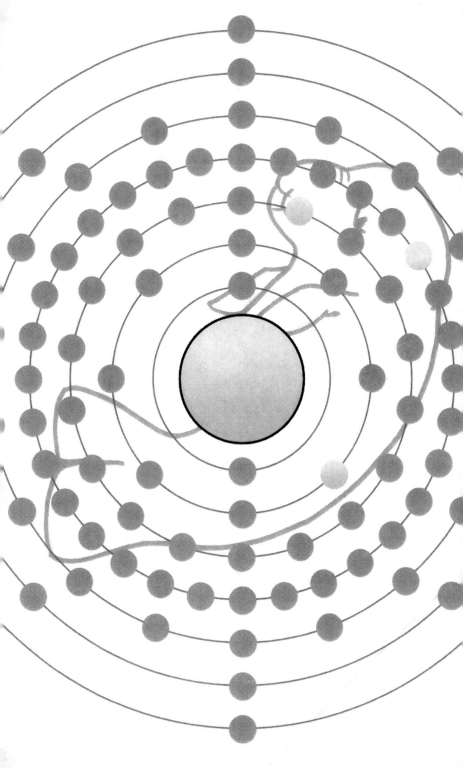

THE PINK MANATEE

Wildflowers are my favorites – you can't really fuck them up, and if you have an off week or two they don't suffer. Daisies, asters, lilies of all kinds. On the arbor Gerald and I built last summer, a wild rose wraps a cautious finger. Perfect order in chaos – I tend it, coax it. When things become too contrived, I stop looking and only plant from the shoe box. In a few weeks it relaxes. Come wintertime, I mark my bulbs and prune back the shrubs, and we till a chunk, stirring the earth and shredding the remains of the year's buried wishes. No one knows I only bury in one section, stirring up the border to the perennials.

"If I had a favorite, would you only plant under that flower?"

"Yes," I answer.

"And if I didn't have any idea, would you just pick a random one or try to choose something that fit?" Charlotte has a secret that she almost but didn't quite leave in the shoe box last night. Dew still heavy on the grass, she picks at her bandaged fingertips when not covering her pocket with both hands.

"It depends. If it was something I thought matched a certain flower, then I would put it there. If not I would plant it near something I thought you would like."

Pushing her hair behind her ears, she smiles. "I have to go in for breakfast. You don't have to?"

Rocking back on my heels, I hand her a yellow day lily on a long stem. "I've been here a long time and I have different privileges. You know how you see Sandra reading outside a lot? She has a flexible schedule, too."

"How long is a long time?"

"For me? Six years, off and on."

"Six years?" Her hands snap at each other, plucking at the band-aids, birds in the air. "It's only been three weeks and it feels like forever. Six years?"

"On and off since I was eighteen. Is that what you want? Out?"

"I want to be done with this." Jazz hands, Charlotte flashes her guilt at me.

Dirt is all I can offer. She pulls a smashed pink box from her pocket. Hard for her to give them up, even these few, mashed with love from being close to her. "Will it work?" Dancing away, nervous.

"It might. It will help. Where?"

Laughing as she runs, "You know where." Charlotte waves the lily I'd cut at random. "You are a witch."

No, but I have the morning to myself again. Squatting in front of the lilies, I stab the ground with my spade. "Charlotte wants to wash her hands in peace." I drop the Barbie band-aids in, humming Dusty Springfield. The shoe box is light - always a good sign.

Seven AM every morning my bare feet hit the grass, and my soles are coated with clean soil before the sun burns off the dew. Filthy to the elbows, petals brushing my face; I would stay in the garden and the morning while the clock spun round and round for infinity.

Wishes from the night before: Amy gave me four earthworms - still likely to survive, with my short turnaround time for spell-casting - and Sandra some bizarre popsicle stick doll - but I plant them all the same. Sandra wants me to plant a popsicle doll with chunks of her hair Elmer's glued to it, in hopes her ovaries will grow back. Why the hell not? She's got a right to dream same as everybody else.

The fevered hand of eastern light on the back of my neck, my fingers twist holes in the dirt and drop the earthworms in. "Amy wants a tunnel out. I know, original." I rummage for Sandra's doll, splintery and gooey and a little brownish – I'd nail it to a post to intimidate imaginary rodents, but if Sandra wants it planted, in the ground it goes. Daisies tickle my ears and daisies forgive everything, so I make a little furrow in their shadow and the doll disappears, headfirst. "Ovaries – again." Warm scalp and shoulders - with all these entrusted treasures, maybe I should wear a gypsy scarf and charms, affirm my credibility. Or work by moonlight. Lifetimes ago I lay under the night sky with a cigarette and an ink pen, but I barely remember that girl.

As for Bridget? Everyone knows Bridget. She'll make your dreams come true.

There is nothing shameful in the perpetuating of false hope. People have so little empathy for brave psychotics like Benny Hinn, standing in front of massive crowds, smacking people on the forehead so thousands at home, alone in the dark – aging, frail, with pictures of Jesus on the wall and a phone that never rings – can dare to believe in miracles. Or Benny Hill, for that matter – old, fat, endlessly chasing strings of beautiful girls. Every ancient man in a recliner with an over-flowing ashtray can aspire to wander into dressing rooms and be rewarded with such good fortune.

So maybe they're not selfless, or even a little pure. Those evangelist guys wear rings like old Mafioso and teeth from primo denture catalogs. They are worshiped. And Benny Hill never really wins; it's always a bit of a cheat. But the point is not lost:

Hope is the point. Unfounded, illogical, life-sustaining hope. The snake oil salesman on the lip of the carriage at the fair – if the bottle's contents cure what ails you, or make you believe it may, what's the harm, really? No one needs an actual cure. Just something to bet on, a twinkle of possibility.

I am the twinkle of possibility around these parts.

Fuck clocks. Fuck the shortening shadows – long before noon the magic is gone. In this rectangle of soil the heliotrope stretch their necks, but my own head droops.

The magic does not last through the day.

Doctors say the meds are to blame – my morning "euphoria" just a leftover high from the pills before bed.

No sensible person could believe anyone that needs a clipboard to feel important - but as ten and eleven inch by, the sound of scratching ink pens and monotone voices hang around my neck like a yoke. Lies are more plausible in a shadowless world.

Tuesdays can be different – and today is Tuesday. Hair pinned to the back of my head, a sundress with pretty ties on my shoulders – the bows represent tentative anticipation, nothing more. Not crossed fingers or anything like that.

Best to be prepared, is all. Never know when a primer grey El Camino will clatter up the House's drive in a cloud of smoke, fractured muffler announcing its arrival long before I can uncurl my spine and shade my eyes with my hand. Half the time it's imagined – a truck on the highway tricks me upright some Tuesdays, with no chariot to cart me away on a day pass from my perfectly ordered plot of soil.

Sweaty and happy and humming at eight AM – I hear it, and it's real. Rumble rumble, Bridget Bridget, it says. My back makes an exclamation point as Eddie lays on the horn. Struck blind; afterimages of too much chrome. Twinkles of possibility. The engine chugs near – he waves the white flag, the Day Pass, from the window and I see it in a strobe effect of rapid blinking – I SURRENDER TO YOU, BRIDGET, the paper might as well say, and it means I am out.

"Princess!" he calls over the groan of the car door – in the corner of my eye Sandra's head snaps up, palms flat on the picnic table across the lawn. A thumbs up flashed in her general direction – the deed is done, the doll is buried, Sandra – she relaxes back into her Dr. Spock.

"I love kidnap," I whisper. A quick glance down at myself reveals 'dressing up' has lost the battle against soil and sun. "Do I need shoes?"

"I can't imagine why you would – we can get you some flippers somewhere if you change your mind." Soft and familiar lips on my neck.

"Flippers? Really?" I push back.

His light eyes and shaggy hair are honest enough, but Eddie's hands betray him. Fingers explore me through my dress, quick as possible, making sure everything is still where he wants it - a cursory frisking that borders on sterile.

"Flip-flops."

"Let me wash my hands." Water from the hose makes a rainbow; it is good to be going. No guilt as the remaining shoebox wishes tumble willy-nilly into a hasty mass garden grave – planted is planted. I press my handprint into the freshly covered mound, and leave my tools and boxes neatly arranged. Wet dress-front and dirty feet, my bare legs make the same squelchy sound every time I scoot onto the car seat.

"I like your hands. They're square and mean." Looking into his palm is reading MAD magazine – a gorgeous combination of lies, satire, and flexible half-truths; on every whorl of sandpaper callous Eddie is etched.

"We can go wherever you want today, do whatever you want," he lies, watching me crank down the window.

Sun on my eyelids, wind in my eyelashes. "Whatever. Let's just do whatever you were planning on doing." Curling toes on the rubber floor mat, This is all I need. Let me be a dog and hang my head from the window all day. I'll be the golden retriever, along for the ride. Just *drive*.

Because we might escape the end of the morning – theoretically, if we drive fast enough, and in the right direction, we can stay in the morning forever. Well, until we go into the ocean. And what better transition? Morning for as long as it can last, then swimming with the mermaids, letting their swirling hair and cool hands walk us down to death, to be planted among the anemone.

Eddie's plan for the day - besides swooping in to snatch the princess from her tower – is stereos. I got no problem with that. Sweating in the car, I spin the knob on the radio and watch he and a fellow who leaves absolutely no impression stack car stereos (with CD players!) in the back. They unfold a blue tarp and strap down the whole aqua mass.

"Don't you have anything less bright?" I call. "That's a really bright tarp. What about khaki or peach or something?"

"Most tarps are blue," Eddie answers. "It's not as conspicuous as you think."

That makes no sense. The window frame sears lines into the undersides of my arms as I mull it over. "What color tarps do they use to cover the dirt piles that they fill in graves with?"

"Blue, I think."

Perfectly satisfactory. I nod, sliding back into the seat. In moments we are back on the road.

"You want the AC on?"

"No, I like the air."

"What did you bury this morning?"

Conversation is payment. He brought me out, after all, to see new things – like fences that are people – so I can't really tell him to shut the fuck up, Dusty Springfield is on and the air smells deliciously of exhaust and mowed grass. Eddie wants foreplay, and this does it for him, as usual.

"Junk. Same as always."

"You believe any of it?"

"Why not? It's all psychosomatic anyway." My hair is undone; I pin it back up with a skeezy ink pen from the floorboard. "Gerald gave me a book of poems – he had gone through and traced the first letter of every sentence in really dark. He wanted me to plant it, to help with his stutter. Now, if he truly believes the garden is magic – that I'm magic, why won't it work? If he believes his stutter is being cured there's a really good chance he'll improve." A thousand times, this conversation. Eddie just wants to hear about crazy people, but doesn't have honesty enough in him to say 'Tell me about the crazies.' "I don't think Sandra's gonna grow her ovaries back with mind power, but knowing she can't have a baby kills her. So the idea that someday if the stars or whatever align right, that she could at least have the necessary parts to make one - that keeps her going."

"She's the one that drowned her baby in the bathtub, right?"

His tone betrays the satisfaction of old news. The shadows nearly non-existent, morning is over.

"You know she is. Fuck you, Eddie. Coulda been an accident."

"In her mind, you mean."

"Well twenty years later how else could it matter, except what's in her mind?"

"What about in your mind?"

"Like in my mind in general? In my mind there's not a whole lot left that's interesting to look at. Popsicle stick dolls, plants that bloom at dark – that stuff is interesting.

The fact that bright blue shiny tarps are somehow inconspicuous, that's interesting." Interesting that Eddie doesn't care who wrote the poems Gerald had me bury.

Interesting what people don't find interesting.

"We're almost there."

"Almost where?" Anger is pointless and fleeting. Eddie explained this excursion to me, but I'm still excited and slightly confused. A fence. A person fence. I can't resolve the images.

The El Camino eases onto a dirty gravel access road parallel to the highway – almost an alley. I can't blame these houses for turning their backs to the interstate. Looking into the backyards of an entire street, my chest tightens to see all these private things. Rusted swing sets, an overturned wading pool, a gas grill; sun burnt ferns hang from an awning, fronds coated in gravel dust. We crawl slowly past. A doll - discarded, just at the edge of the road. I look directly into her blue eyes, my fingers grope for the door handle.

"Don't you dare!" Eddie hisses.

Rage flashes again for a split second, but I can't keep it in focus. Maybe while he talks to the fence I can sneak away and steal the doll, take it back to Sandra to be loved and cleaned – instead of lying in a jumble of limbs and tangled hair.

Eddie brakes at the rear of a cinder block building, once white, with what can only be a peeling pink ....manatee on the side. "What the fuck." We creep past the decrepit sea mammal, Eddie cranking the wheel right and inching into the drive. The garage door is pushed all the way up and looking into the dark interior is a difficult adjustment, especially after such a huge pink manatee.

In the negative space of the garage crouches a car in a state of disembowelment. It is precisely barely inside - I am positive a string hung from the top of the doorway would brush fibers against its rusty front bumper. Circling it in a wide arc, stepping into the day, is the human fence.

He wears blue jeans and a white t-shirt, wiping his hands on a rag. The sun hits him full in the face and he squints into the light - up into it.

And my fingers and toes go numb, my lips and tongue, the only sensation left is that of a hand closing around my throat.

He is the most beautiful thing I have ever seen.

Black hair combed straight back, like a half-ass Elvis impersonator - like he wanted to do it, but lost his train of thought and wandered away from the mirror. For a split-second I see a pack of Lucky Strikes rolled in his sleeve but it's my imagination. He raises a hand in greeting and I realize the El Camino has stopped, almost nose to nose with the black one. "Holy Jesus Christ in Heaven."

"Are you getting out?" Eddie props his door open with his ratty sneaker, the human fence person wiping his hands, watching.

"Is that him?"

"Yeah, come on."

"Are we in the 1950's? Did we time travel? Is that possible?" My fingers wake up one by one, wrapped around my kneecaps.

"Don't get crazy on me now, Bridget. You can wait in

the car or you can get out and play normal."

"Oh I'm fucking getting out. I'm getting out." Unable to look away from the new creature, I scramble free of the car, somehow arriving at the front of the El Camino in sync with Eddie. For the first time I can recall, I wish I had worn shoes.

The sun directly overhead, I stare.

His eyes are dark, they smile even when he does not, and even when he does not want them to, I would guess. They draw light, absorb it, and reveal – what would be the right word? Bemusement. That may be right. The motion of his hands is thinking movement, much like nail-biting or chin-stroking; the rag is a clever prop. He and Eddie begin to talk, and I tell myself to stop looking at his blackened nail beds and try to pay attention, join the conversation.

Bravery. This is a moment where bravery is important. Oh, and something dramatic. Drama, drama – with only soap operas on the rec room television as a reference point, I take the pen from my hair, letting it fall in a chaotic mess to my shoulders.

A sideways glance, not the effect I hoped for. His mind is elsewhere, his attention stays on Eddie. Looking past him into the garage, I swallow everything in gulping breaths – the phone bolted to the wall, the rags on the table next to a dusty radio - the knobs clean – an open door at the back revealing a slice of room: bare bulb, mirror, white porcelain sink. I want to dart past him and put my hands all over these things – flip on the radio to see what songs come out, push redial on the phone, shuffle through his magazines, wash my hands in his sink, dig in all the greasy grimy nuts and bolts and things that are everywhere. Mingle my fingerprints with his until they're indistinguishable. The car is almost unrecognizable, hood up; the few things left inside naked to the world.

Oh, the car and I – we are the same, I exhale to keep from blushing.

Eddie's jittery laugh wakes me enough to pull myself with force into the moment – I do not want to forever be the crazy barefoot girl that showed up one afternoon, unremarkable and never to be seen again.

"Is that a manatee?" 'Manatee' is an attention grabber. Noted for future reference. My toes curl under his gaze. "On the side of the building. A big pink manatee?"

Miracle of miracles, he smiles. Mouth closed, the right side of his mouth higher than the other. His eyes crinkle at the corners; he squints to soften eye contact – I get it. "Yeah, I think so. I think this place used to be a bar." He puts out his hand, sideways.

Mine slips into his without brain-to-hand permission. It's dirty and exciting – I go slowly, skimming his palm with my fingertips, unsure I will be able to let go after an appropriate sliver of time. His squeeze is a swift clench and unclench, my knees go squirrely, the squeeze in my belly and my eyes. "I'm Bridget." Tiny voice, not mine. Weird. "If I had known we were coming to see you, I would have worn shoes."

"Not a problem. I'm Max. Nice to meet you." Behind the squint are unreadable things; he is accustomed to hiding.

I can almost see past his eyelashes, into his skull, almost hear the gears turning, almost see the things he is thinking….

"Nice to meet you, too. You have lovely hands. You're the first fence I ever met."

His eyes widen with a surprised laugh, and I involuntarily lean forward to look deeper. My toes are practically spasming. The El Camino's bumper against the back of my thighs stops the vertigo, and ever so slowly I unclasp my fingers. His calluses are smooth, polished stones - carved hands, no detail overlooked. Perfect.

"Where did you find her?" Max's mouth recovers from the smile more quickly than his eyes, it disappears from even the corners of his lips as he looks me up and down, quick.

Alarm in Eddie's face. His embarrassment in admitting he semi-regularly bangs an institutionalized female is the most constant thing about him. "She was roommates with my sister for about a year and a half."

Technically this is true. Until Mandy Lynn slit her wrists in the arts and crafts room, but Eddie never stopped visiting the place. He always leaves the end off the story.

"Is there a little girl about four houses down?" I ask.

Eddie shoots eye daggers at me, but if I'm lucky the day will reward me with a doll if not an orgasm.

"Yeah, her name's Maggie."

"She yours?"

Max knits his eyebrows.

Too much. Gotta be careful and speak like other people.

"No," he answers.

"Could I go talk to her?"

The muscles in his shoulders stretch his t-shirt when he shrugs, and he leans back against the gutted and helpless car. "Guess so. Don't think Eddie's gonna make you help us unload."

Escape. Four steps and I am out from under his eyes and I can breathe, wrenching the noose from my neck. The gravel presses acupuncture points in the bottoms of my feet leading directly to my chest, and a layer of dust settles over the layer of dirt. I stop at the doll, calling "Maggie! Maggie, you home?" Far to my left, the blue tarp disappears; Eddie and Max carry stacks of boxes inside.

"Yeah?"

She might be seven, with her blond ponytail, Wonder Woman bathing suit and flip-flops. Cautious, ten feet away in the yard. Smart.

Picking the doll up by a grimy leg, I ask if it's hers.

"Nah, my cousin left it here. I don't like it. She wrote all over it."

Spinning the doll, I hadn't noticed before. Some twisted kid drew stitches all over the damned thing with a sharpie. This was more perfect for Sandra than I thought. "Okay if I take it?"

"Whatever." Maggie tries to hold in her curiosity by folding her skinny arms across her chest, something most people do to hide the beginnings of thoughts.

"Thanks. I'm Bridget. Just stopping to see Max."

"You are? You're not Max's girlfriend."

I mimic her arm-folding. "How do you know?"

She snorts with authority; I like her a lot. "Cause I

seen her. She's got bleachy hair and is sorta skanky. Always wears stupid shoes."

"Stupid how?"

"Pointy, bright – like the plastic ones that come in princess sets but for grown-ups, you know?"

I answer with an understanding nod.

"You his new girlfriend?"

"Not yet."

Maggie giggles. "I like your dress."

"I like your bathing suit. It was nice to meet you."

"Yeah," she grins and means it, waving as I walk away. "Hey Bridget, when you come back wear shoes – sometimes there's glass in the road."

"Okay. Thanks for the doll! Hey Maggie?"

"Yeah?"

"What's skanky?"

Giggling again, she does a cartwheel for me. "Like slutty. Like bleachy hair and stupid shoes!"

"Okay. Bye!"

Waving, Maggie shoots across the yard; I hear the screen slam behind her.

Light and dark, Eddie and Max face each other in the sun leaning against their respective vehicles. Eddie's posture is a bit off; he eyes the filthy baby under my arm.

"Maggie said I could have it. I didn't just take it."

"You took the doll?" Max's eyebrows arch again. His shoulders relax as I approach, he digs in his jeans pocket for what I know to be a book of matches. He wouldn't have a lighter, not a cheap plastic one, anyway. A cigarette dangles from his lips and I focus on it to keep my eyes from darting: mouth, crotch, mouth, crotch.

"No, I just said, I didn't take it, she gave it to me." I toss it through the open car window. "It's for Sandra." For Eddie's imaginary reputation: "A girl that lives in my building. She's a fixer-upper type."

"Do you have shoes in the car?" Max smokes with his chin in his hand, one eye squinted, looking at me.

Looking at me.

Eddie's eyes jump back and forth between us.

"No."

"You came all this way with no shoes?"

"I came all this way with no shoes, no purse, no ID, no tattoos – if we died in a wreck on the way home it could take weeks and possibly dental records to identify me." Shit. I have no idea how to talk to a normal person. But how normal is this Max fence? He looks like a displaced 50's greaser. He just took possession of like a hundred hot stereos. Too late anyway, already said it and it must be okay, because he laughs.

"You're crazy."

Eddie snorts. "You have no idea."

"My girl can't go down the block without luggage. She's got like, a million pairs of shoes, and all of them with heels like this," He spreads his thumb and forefinger. "And you - no shoes, no purse, nothing." He smiles again. "You look very pretty, though. I wasn't insulting you."

"Thank you. I'm like a sex offender's wet dream." My fear melts quickly as a general rule, and if he keeps talking to me like I am a normal person, and laughing, the chances are good I will wrap my limbs around him, not to be removed without a taser. "Your girlfriend short?"

"Sorta, yeah."

Mocking Maggie's knowing face, I nod as if that makes sense. Tracing a line with my toe through the dust between Max and me, about an inch from the round end of his work boot, I inadvertently draw all eyes to my bare foot and how dangerously close I am to revealing myself.

"I can find shoes you like."

"What?" Eddie and I ask simultaneously.

"You bring her back, Eddie. When you two usually run around?" His eyes flit over Eddie and a muscle in his jaw tenses for a split second. I file this.

"Tuesdays," I answer for him.

"Perfect – you gotta come back next week anyway, Ed, come back Tuesday and bring Bridget with you. You," he points his cigarette at me before flicking it away. "You I have figured out."

Eddie runs a hand across his mouth and a cloud crosses his eyes. "Alright, you say so. Tuesday." I can hear the wheels spinning, quick enough to produce sparks. He touches his back pocket, his phone. "Can I use your john?"

Max nods.

Eddie disappears into the hole of the garage while I stand barefoot, nearly naked, opposite what may be the most beautiful human being in the living world.

"Can I see your foot?"

"What?" Almost a squeak, and it shames me.

Palm up, Max puts out his hand. "Your foot."

"It's dirty."

Spreading his fingers, "So are my hands."

Sliding my foot into his hand is even better than the handshake, and what I imagine sex to be like - the kind in movies and on TV and in books. My throat catches in that cliché way and my stomach flips and my other leg nearly goes out from under me.

Better than I thought it would be. Studying it like a piece of clockwork, or more likely a car part of some type, his hand moves like fluid stone – not soft but smooth. Brown highlights in his hair, not as black as I thought. I absorb everything I can – the tendons in his neck, the dirty knees of his jeans, his eyelashes.

"You Eddie's girl?" He doesn't look up. His opposite hand comes up, almost touches my ankle, changes its mind and disappears again.

"No."

"Does he know that?"

"Never really thought about it."

Max smiles, flattening his palm, the brush of his fingers disappearing all at once. I put my foot back in the dust, tingling.

"Is the 50's thing what they call a 'look'?"

"What 50's thing?"

"Could I have a cigarette?"

With a deep breath he holds out the pack, but I've begun to catch on – he wants to see if I'll lean into it, take it from the pack with my mouth. After the foot-touching thing – I think about what Maggie told me, and remove one delicately with my fingers. Lighting it with a paper match, his face is like a satisfied cat's.

"There are a lot of games to all this, it's incredibly complicated." A genuine sigh escapes with my admission, and in the split-second before he breaks eye contact, Max looks surprised.

"You say awfully honest things to a stranger."

A while since I had a cigarette, it is delicious. My shoulders lower half an inch. "I also take toys from the side of the road."

For perhaps sixty seconds we are silent, studying each other through and around the things we don't say.

Eddie emerges from the shadows. "Ready, Bridget?"

"Sure." Resisting the urge to put both arms around Max, I flick away the cigarette to extend only my hand, one more time. "It was wonderful to meet you."

"You, too." Max looks sideways at Eddie. "I'll see you guys next Tuesday." He folds both hands around mine and I feel it in my thighs.

Gliding to the car is like being on the old meds. I hold the foot of the doll in my hand on the ride back, face in the wind, not caring why Eddie is so quiet.

The blanket billows as Eddie spreads it, red raft on a green sea of grass. This park is the Sex Park. Most people call it Fairmount Park – like on the sign – and kids under ten call it Duck Park because of the evil fowl that chase the picnickers mercilessly in gangs, demanding crusts and onion rings.

On Tuesdays it is the El Camino's last stop before returning me to my walled neighborhood of eccentrics. A Day Pass tradition, Eddie fills me full of cheeseburger and chocolate shake, then I lie on my back with my dress around my waist and he fills a condom full of fantasies about movie stars.

Rolling off me, he flings the guilty balloon into the bushes as the teenagers do and joins me in looking at the sky. It's spectacular, full of kindergarten drawings of clouds; the breeze pushes our shadows across the blades of grass, flicking at the dark edges to lengthen them. Usually this is the best part, the after-time, the silence.

"You need to be careful."

His voice never this quiet, my interest is piqued. Up on one elbow, I prompt him with rapid-fire blinks.

"I saw you look at Max, and that's okay. But – but he's not this nice… whatever you think he is."

"Why not? He could be."

"But he isn't. This stuff - I have a few things left to do before I can get out from under Max."

Of course that makes me giggle.

"Bridget! You don't get it. I owe this guy, like not - it would take like a year to explain even the words to you –"

"I'm not stupid."

"Of course you're not stupid. But it's a long story. I was hoping to have a little longer than Tuesday to get all my shit straightened out–"

"This is getting boring." Rolling onto my back, a vulture circles – interesting, in conjunction with the conversation.

"You don't have to be so goddamned honest all the time!"

"I can't help it." The vulture's loops are patient as opposed to lazy. It draws me back to Max and I shudder. "Eddie, are we dating?"

"Oh come on, Bridget. Now really isn't the time to get into – I mean, we have lives that just…. Well, our relationship – and yes, I consider it a relationship, of a certain kind…" The words fall out of his mouth in a practiced stumbling way – he already had this conversation in his head. I am not disturbed, only surprised.

"It's okay, Eddie, I don't want to have some weird relationship talk with you, like girlfriends do. I just wanted to make sure one thing was clear."

"And what is that?" He zips his pants, his voice bitter.

"Don't drip your sarcasm on me."

"That is the thing you needed to make clear?" Wadding the blanket with frantic hands, his face just as red.

"I'm not your girl."

"No, Bridget, you're not my girl." The vulture is gone and Eddie's guilt is heavier on my skin than the muggy afternoon. "Bridget, I have a girlfriend. Her name is Kate. And no, she doesn't know about you, how could she? We've been dating almost four months, and I'm not sure where it's going, but you...." His pained confession comes rolling out, I bite my cheeks to keep from smiling. "You're... well, you're Bridget. And I don't want to give you up. You are my sister's best friend-"

"Was your sister's best friend." I make my voice cold.

"Oh Bridget, I'm sorry. God I'm an idiot. Can we talk about this some other time? I know it's important, but I have to figure out..."

Not sure how much longer he apologizes, I fade out by the time we're back in the car.

Hard to believe how many interesting things can happen in just one day.

I love Tuesdays.

"You're a sociopath." Sandra drags the brush through my hair with whiplash strokes, same angle as the row of wind chimes that reach sideways, rattling like bones. The three of us are the only ones left on the porch; it's near dark and they'll call us in soon and make sure we get to our appropriate rooms.

I've just finished the story of Eddie's girlfriend. "That's not what Dr. Mengele says. He says – well, something different every week. He knows I'm not going anywhere."

Charlotte and Sandra giggle. Sandra, at least, is like

me: appreciative of a charmed existence.

Ungrateful brats come and go in this place – of all ages, shapes, sizes. They can't seem to make it work out there, but think of this place as "locked up". But almost any of the permanents could tell you how much worse it can be – most of us have been in other "facilities". Lots of other facilities. The ones that look like hospitals or prisons, staffs of curious doctors with free rein to try and "fix" the patients.

This place? A resort by comparison. And we all have benefactors - represented by trusts, or family payment plans, or, for some like me, connections - that pay dearly and in full so that we can sit at dusk on a wraparound porch, watching the light disappear before we are escorted to safe, comfortable beds.

Guilt pays for everything. Guilt keeps the staff understanding and the doctors laid back and the kitchen smelling wholesome – the same way that hope keeps the residents (for the most part) patient and calm, and satisfied as a bunch of lunatics could be.

"Done!" Charlotte holds up Emma – the doll from Maggie's yard – for both of us to see.

Amazing what a bit of attention will do for a lump of plastic. With a clean dress and combed hair, Emma was greatly improved – but Charlotte put on the perfecting touches: each and every sharpie wound is carefully dressed with a Barbie band-aid.

"Oh Charlotte," Sandra hugs the doll to her heart and strokes the back of its head like I imagine any mother would. "You should have been a nurse, dear."

Charlotte is nineteen and beams when happy, even

in the dimmest light. She tucks dark hair behind her ears with hands also covered with Barbie band-aids.

A shadow in the shape of a woman falls through the doorway and we all rise.

Wednesday afternoon is Arts & Crafts or Church. For a while Sandra was on a church kick, but soon realized she was missing out on what amounted to a sewing circle, though needles of any kind are of course strictly forbidden. As well as X-acto knives and pretty much anything that can make large gouges.

Mandy Lynn didn't die totally in vain - and was far from forgotten. Every time someone tries to cut mat board with safety scissors, you can hear them mutter: "Damn you, Mandy Lynn."

Summer is Sculpey season – no one wants to use an oven in this heat. For weeks we mash and bend and curse our way through occupational therapy on the terrace adjoining the studio – gossiping, bitching, occasionally creating art or witnessing a meltdown.

In short, Arts & Crafts is the loony bin version of the high school lunch room, but every table is the cool kids' table.

My cool kids' table seats four since Mandy Lynn swam in blood and glitter to the Great Beyond, but this is a week of change. Sandra, wearing Baby Emma in a sling, drags Charlotte behind her by one bandaged hand.

Three sets of eyes look up; Charlotte is pale as

a ghost. She must've gone to real high school, must understand this concept of peer rejection and acceptance on some level besides ridiculous.

"I believe you've met most of us, but I'm not sure you've been properly introduced," Sandra's back is stiff with decorum. "Gerald is a poet. Amy can spell any word you ever need to spell. I'm the mom, and as you know, Bridget is the witch."

"Sandra's seen the Breakfast Club too many times," Amy mutters, and when we all laugh – Sandra included – Charlotte falls with relief into a chair and into our circle, and after almost two years, Mandy Lynn is formally replaced.

The topic over Sculpey is Romeo and Juliet. I pick up where I left off. "I didn't say I didn't believe in love at first sight. I just don't see what that has to do with Romeo and Juliet – okay, to be perfectly honest, I'm only familiar with the Shakespeare version and all its diluted movie versions, and not the original folk story. That might have been about love at first sight for all I know. I jumped to a conclusion, there."

"No, you're correct in your assumption," Gerald's voice is quiet and careful; he usually thinks awhile about what he wants to say to mentally drive out the stutter – like driving out a demon. When he speaks everyone listens. We all turn to him - tiny, bald and absorbed in the delicate act of attaching perfect petals to what is becoming a rose. "And everything you describe about this encounter sss-seems - to me - very much like Romeo and Juliet."

"But Romeo and Juliet wasn't about love at first sight, it was about a rebound turning into forbidden fruit which is the tastiest fruit of all. And maybe I did fall in love with a mechanic when I first saw him. I'm really not sure, only that I never feel drawn to or connected to humans outside here – but I was drawn to him." My white ball takes on the proportions of a penis – I gouge in eyes and use my thumbnail to make a crescent smile.

"Precisely," Gerald's eyes widen. "You, Romeo, in the throes of your...whatever...with Rosalind - Eddie, of course - meet someone entirely different, and entirely off-limits, cloaked in the outside world as he is," he holds the bent rose out to me. "Max is your Juliet."

"Jesus," Charlotte breathes, "You're smart."

I accept the rose with lifted brows. "I'm stealing your theory to use with Dr. Matthews tomorrow morning. As long as I'm mooning in fairy tale land, he keeps giving me day passes."

"Why?"

"Because, Charlotte," I hand off the rose to her and steeple my fingers, looking into her eyes over them in my Dr. Matthews imitation.

Amy molds a pistol, half-grinning and shaking her head.

"I'm searching for context, filters through which to make sense of the world. I'm making progress."

Four out of five of us laugh. Charlotte stares at her untouched block of Sculpey.

"It's not cynicism, dear," Sandra places a hand over one of Charlotte's, the doll cradled in her other arm.

"Yes it is."

"Hush, Amy."

Amy points her floppy pistol at Sandra.

The penis disappears under my fist. "The only way to keep from going crazy - did I just say that?" This time Charlotte does laugh with us. "The only way to make it work with the doctors is to try and accept that their only framework for any of *this*..." I put my fingertip on her forehead, "comes from textbooks. It doesn't always work, but it's important not to yell when they talk to you like a kindergartener."

My big fucking mouth, spoiling all the Zen of Institutionalization. My hubris. False wisdom. Easier said than done. Other cliches.

"I fuck Eddie because I don't mind and it makes us even for the other things we do on days out – I don't like to owe people."

The glasses shield him from eye contact without betraying this avoidance. "His chin drops to glance over his doodles. "You don't want to 'owe anyone' as you put it – but you don't mind others being indebted to you. Why?"

There is a spot on the wall above the window, a nail hole where Phyllis – this was her office maybe four, five years ago, before she died – had tacked a handwritten copy of the Serenity Prayer. Focusing on it, on the hole and the prayer still hidden inside it, I bite down on blossoming anger at his thickness. "No one owes me anything for the garden. If you haven't noticed I get quite a lot of help with the work. As for the other stuff, I do that because I want to."

"Do you think it helps?"

It seems like a trap, so I keep my mouth shut.

"Why do you think Sandra's doctor let her keep the doll you brought?"

"Why do you think I let your predecessor have sex with me?"

"The two subjects have nothing to do with each other, and I won't let you draw us off topic by bringing up something potentially volatile."

"Sometimes I think you're provoking me on purpose. I'm not sure if you're leading me or I'm leading you."

"Did you think engaging in a sexual relationship with Dr. White would guarantee you a female counselor when the affair was discovered?"

Tap, tap, tap, tap – sometimes I have to stare at my fingers to remind them who is boss. After a deep breath, I answer. "The doll makes her happy, and doesn't do any harm to anyone." My hand is involuntarily at my lips; I grip the armrest again. I will not bite my fingernails. "It's the same reason I had sex with Dr. White. It made him happy, and it wasn't hurting anyone."

"It wasn't hurting anyone?"

"It wasn't hurting anyone, that's what I said. Could I have a glass of water, please?"

"Of course." There is a mini-fridge in his office, same as all the others. Same beige carpet, same cream mini-blinds, same sage green walls. When Phyllis was here she replaced the crispy-looking valances with lacy things, and dressed the furniture with soft pillows. Her desk had an anniversary clock with a glass dome over it instead of the standard psychiatrist ball-swinging doo-hicky that Mengele has.

A red patch appears on the back of my hand before I realize I'm scratching, but I remember to thank him for the water before draining it. "I assumed I would get a female counselor, yes. But that had nothing to do with motive. The motives weren't mine. It just didn't seem to interfere with the progress we weren't making." The idea is for him to shuffle papers, become confused, jump from subject to subject, chase my train of thought. But afternoons make me a slow rabbit.

"Would you rather have rescheduled our session today?"

What I thought had been a reprieve had actually been a lie. Whether a calculated lie or an honest mistake, I've yet to determine. At 9:45A.M. Amy brought a note to me in the garden, a schedule amendment scribbled on a paper from the secretary's official Helm Grove notepads. It said, "Fuck your afternoon nap, your doctor is busy and you have to be in his office at 2pm instead of in fifteen minutes. Everything we told you about sticking to schedules is just to make things convenient for the staff. Fuck you." When I'd read my version of the note's contents Amy had laughed.

"Are you kidding? Two o'clock is the hour striking continuously in hell." Swirling the ice in the glass I look up, calmly, as calmly as possible. "Yes, I would rather have rescheduled your reschedule."

"Do you want to talk about why you feel that way?"

"Do you think I want to talk about it? Jesus Christ. How much longer?"

"We've only been talking twenty minutes."

Twenty minutes. Twenty minutes. I close my eyes, thinking about passing Charlotte in the hall on my way here, and how big her smile was. Just for taking some of her band-aids, and giving her a flower, a seat at my table. This is a good place. These are good people. The doctors are just doing their jobs, even if most of the time they do them badly. The roses started to bloom this morning, one small pink bud unfolding, and somewhere less than two hours away a beautiful creature promised me shoes. Just like in Cinderella. Well, not just like in Cinderella. But best to keep all this in a fairy tale framework while I'm stuck in this office.

Opening my eyes, I release a sigh I would rather have kept to myself.

"Bridget."

"If you tell me to calm down I will smash your stupid glass bird- I hate that fucking thing. Sip, sip, sip. An organ grinder's monkey would be more encouraging – and if I were any more calm I would be in a coma."

"Bridget, there are only two female counselors on staff. Do you know why I'm telling you this?"

"To fill up time?"

"You have already had an unsuccessful counseling relationship with one of the female doctors, and the other is Sandra's counselor, and thinks she may be conflicted were she to work with you. She's very close to Sandra."

I answer through my eyelids. "I know. Sandra loves her."

"There were no female counselors to take your case. It was given to me because I was the available doctor with the least in common with Dr. White."

Dr. White had wide grey eyes, didn't wear glasses. Looked lost most of the time, his folders were a mess, he could never find a pen. He mixed up names. Flirted with nurses. He hadn't deserved Phyllis's office.

Sometimes it's easiest to tell the truth, even if the truth makes no difference. "He was Mandy Lynn's doctor. I wanted him to lose his job. I had to fuck that bastard for six months before we got caught."

I open my hand, watching my water glass thump the floor. I know it makes no sense, but my belly and lungs still burn when there's no smash. Sometimes things need to break before you feel any relief. My leg shoots straight out - like my knee was whacked with a hammer – and I bend it quickly.

The glass makes a delicate scream under my bare heel as it caves, in perfect sync with the sensation of a tiny fire. I exhale a plume of invisible smoke, well before Dr. Mengele reaches his desk phone.

Four stitches and twenty-four hours' observation. The nurse is a big black guy everybody calls Barney, like Hannibal Lecter's nurse. His face is just covered by a paperback copy of *The Master and Margarita*, slouching in a chair outside the open door.

"That book's a bunch of shit," I call. Sleepy drugged voice, the least favorite of all my voices. This part of the house looks like a hospital; I wear a gown with snaps and leave the door open when I go to the bathroom. All fluorescents, except the little lamp bolted to the bolted-down nightstand. Mauve walls, the hum of electricity. The hum makes me think of Chief Broom, of being too young to understand the beauty of *Let It Be* by the Beatles.

Shameful to be here at all. Haven't laid eyes on this hallway in over a year.

"You could just say 'Hi.'" Barney smiles, dog-earing the page and leaving the book in his chair. We've both been at this too long to be self-conscious of the camera in the corner. He hands me a plastic cup of water and maneuvers himself into the plastic chair against the wall. "You been awake long?"

"Yeah, I'm stewing in my own shame."

"It's only four stitches, this is just protocol. Dr. Michaels said he let the session get out of control. Plus he gave you a glass made out of *glass*. He's not a bad guy."

The bed sounds as if it is digesting me while rising. "I know he's not." My feet make a white tent at the end of the bed. "Just protocol?"

"Yeah, any act of self-inflicted – shit, you know the drill. They know you weren't trying to make a dramatic exit, but you stomped a fucking drinking glass. That's a mandatory sedation and night in the neon ward." Barney yawns. "You really read that book?"

I giggle. "Yeah, it's actually really good." Sitting up really kicks in the extra gravity of the IV. "Charlotte been down this way this week?"

"Bridget, you know I can't tell you about other patients." He rubs the outer corner of his eye with two fingers – one means yes, two means no.

I smile. Charlotte's a good girl. I want her to stick around – in every sense. "Sorry, Barney. Drugs make me curious." The rectangle of fluorescent above me is the exact opposite of my garden, and my garden is the exact opposite of a grave – which logically means fluorescent lights are perfect facsimiles of graves. "I met a boy. I might be in love."

"Oh, Bridget, say it ain't Eddie."

We both chuckle, and for a split second I harbor undeserved sympathy for Eddie.

"No… like a real boy. Like Brando. He's beautiful."

"Another 'mechanic'?"

Barney could be a real sport about speaking in code. We share another chuckle.

I shrug, or try to.

"Can I give you some advice?"

"Would you consider yourself well-adjusted?"

"Not even close."

"Then by all means, advise me."

"You're a good girl, Bridget. Don't think just because you're in here you should take whoever will have you. You're more than this place."

Rolling my head along the pillow, I offer a lazy smile. "Jesus, when did you get all insightful and shit?"

"I've been in the self-help section of the library. I'm turning my life around."

Another shared laugh, it drowns out the electric

buzz.

We got here the same week, Barney and me. Got to know each other in a room not much different than this – and it may very well be my fault he gets called Barney. Twisted that the better I do the less I see him.

"Dammit , Barney, I wanted to talk, but the knock out drops are taking me down again."

"I'll be here all night. Yell if you need anything."

I might be nodding, but he is using the button to make the bed flat.

"Goodnight, Bridget." He flips off the light on his way out, settles back into his book before I go dark.

⁕

"It's like he missed the malpractice classes or something - everybody knows the patient is always wrong. We had to do one of those shitty full-panel meetings when they released me from Neon yesterday, and he said he let the session get out of hand, there were too many trigger subjects being addressed at the same time."

"Obviously he's new to this or he would never have done something like that," Gerald says, handing over the shoebox. "It's sort of flattering – to you, I mean – that they gave you to him as a patient."

"How's that?" The box is light. I give it a shake.

"New doctors only get simple cases - no one problematic or violent. No one like Amy," he smiles as I scoop out the all-too-familiar earthworms.

Put that way, it is sort of flattering. "As far as I can tell none of my privileges have been taken away. Eddie put in for the day pass paperwork yesterday, right on schedule, and it was approved, I checked at the office." Sliding backwards off my toes, I land on my butt in the soft dirt instead of my heels. Stupid stitches. "It doesn't feel like Saturday. I feel like I blinked and lost the whole week." I let my body relax, stretching back into the grass, arms above my head. The sun is warm on my eyelids, the grass cool on my shoulders. Like floating. "We should get some of those pink lilies, the ones without leaves - naked ladies - for next spring. Let's look in the catalogs this evening, see when we need to order bulbs."

I can hear Gerald sigh, hear the stab of his spade in the earth.

"Tell me, Dad. What's on your mind?" For a second my stomach twists, I'm afraid he's realized his book of poems isn't still in the ground. Seemed a shame to let e.e. cummings rot, and thinking he'd realize this later, I'd snuck the book back out of the ground Wednesday and back up to my room -

"Bridget, you're not making sense."

I wait. In the distance I hear Charlotte and Sandra laugh from Sandra's customary picnic table. It's a good sound.

"Eddie I understand. He's a distraction, and he understands us, this place, all of it. But you and your J-J-Juliet..." Another sigh. "What does he know about you and here? If we had a place Out There, we'd *be* out there."

"Thinking ahead is not my strong suit, Gerald. Eddie is wearing on me. Just because I leave with him doesn't mean I forgive him, or have any sort of affection for him, no matter what he thinks." My stomach is sour, and my hands are shaky when I push myself up. "I just like to leave sometimes. And he's the only person I've got to take me."

"Sometimes," Gerald pushes his glasses up with a dirty finger and pulls the spade from the ground, nodding a little sadly. "You treat the real world like a theme park."

Lifting my eyebrows, I put my temple on the heel of my hand. "It is. This place is who I am."

We turn our heads simultaneously, our eyes following the lawn that rolls down and away from the House, the garden, down the hill to the tall, wrought-iron fence that wraps around our two acres. The fence keeps us safe from the world, keeps the world safe from us.

"I haven't wanted anything in a long time, Gerald."

"Neither have I. Maybe it scares me that you do, I'm a little afraid you'll..."

He's most likely to stutter on words he's afraid to say, and sometimes skips them altogether. "Run?" I ask.

Nodding, I watch him smile at the fence. "It's a gilded cage we live in," his voice is softer even than before. "Best to never forget we're broken birds."

On Tuesday morning, Eddie's face is not the usual face I see in the El Camino – he's cranky and distracted. This pick-up is obviously because my presence was requested, and very much fucking with his sense of control.

But whatever. Window down, oldies up, and the signed paperwork on the seat between us says Free Till Sundown.

Twenty minutes into the ride he notices I'm wearing shoes. Just in time to ruin Sam Sham's *Little Red Riding Hood*.

"Stepped on some glass, had to get stitches."

"Stepped on or stomped on?"

"So how's Kate, Eddie? You guys catch a movie, bang in the back of the car, any of that typical date-type stuff over the weekend?" My toes want to curl around each other but can't – Charlotte wrangled me into some sort of open toe slip-on sandal contraptions with heels that slap the ground, making me sound like a galloping horse when I walk.

"What would you know about typical dates, Bridget? They don't have prom in the asylums."

Actually it's pretty funny. Rubbing my face in both hands, I ask if this is how it has to be now.

"Fuck, I don't know. I got no clue what's going on. To be honest, if Max hadn't pretty much ordered me to bring you back, I'm really not sure whether I'd have come by today or not."

Sometimes Eddie forgets the difference between crazy and stupid. He doesn't see me roll my eyes. "You get everything straightened out, though? I mean, he's not gonna shoot you or anything, right? I need a ride back."

"It's not funny. You could at least try not to smile when you say stuff like that. Just don't grab your ankles the second we get there, okay?"

"Same to you."

Eddie jumps at his ringing phone, fumbling it open. A thirty second conversation of affirmatives before he tosses the cell between us and begins to mutter "Fuck," over and over.

"What?"

Shaking his head, eyes cloudy. "It'll be fine. Just too many things in one day. If everything lines up I'll be golden. If not I may end up with more bullet holes." After agitated to a certain point, Eddie lapses into melodrama and his seriousness becomes impossible to measure.

Same dusty gravel road, same ache of loneliness just cruising along it. Passing Maggie's yard I blurt, "Stop here! I'll catch up."

"What? What do you mean you'll catch up?"

"Gotta talk to Maggie." I rustle the grocery bag he failed to notice.

"Well hurry up."

"Just do your thing, Eddie. I'll be there in a minute." Slamming the door, I march – or try, in the stupid sandals – to the edge of the road, the El Camino puttering the rest of the way to the manatee.

"Maggie! Hey, Maggie!"

"You stepped on glass, didn't you?" Surprised and overjoyed to be right, Maggie nearly skips across the yard, just an oversized She-Ra t-shirt and stick legs. Her face makes the appropriate polite change; by the time she reaches me her mouth is turned downward in concern. "I stepped on glass once, too. Hurt to walk for like *ever*. Does it hurt bad?"

"No, I just suck at walking in shoes. They make me look drunk, and I feel like I'm going to fall up."

"Fall up?"

"Fall some way. Here, my friend Sandra sent you this." I push the bag at her and her mouth shrinks to a tiny line.

"Why?"

"Because you let me take her the doll, and she doesn't have any daughters of her own, and because she's good at making stuff and spends pretty much all her time doing it. Here." Swinging it does the trick; she snatches the white pendulum and pulls out a yellow sundress.

"Really? She made it?" Holding it up; her mouth tries on different emotions but her eyes read plain old shocked. Around careful clothespin fingers she looks at my own dress.

"Yup. Told ya, she likes to make stuff." Holding the edges of my skirt, I do a little pose and Maggie smiles. Besides the fact that mine is slightly larger and lipstick red, they're identical. Pretty sure Sandra only has one pattern.

"You tell her thank you, okay? Tell her Maggie said thank you." Staring at the little dress, her mouth still working - I wonder where her parents are, what she does for fun, what her life is like – but I've got no room, no room for her in my head. "Hey, you goin' to see Max?"

"On my way."

"You be there long?"

"Not a clue." Oh, I hope so, I hope so, I hope we're

here all day and I get to stare at him and put my hands on his hands and – well, put my hands on anything of his. The jitter comes over me. Fuck Eddie and his waste of agitation – butterflies should be relished.

"Well hey, I'll come down in a little bit, to give you something – for her I mean. What's her name?"

"Sandra."

"Okay. You stop here before you leave if I don't get down there first, okay?"

"Sure."

"Promise, Bridget?" Maggie looks like a little kid with her head tilted like that.

"Promise." I smile. "I won't leave this street without seeing you first."

"Okay." Breaking into a huge grin a split-second before she breaks into a run, I weaken for a moment, wondering why the ferns are dead.

I clomp in the direction of that fat ugly sea cow, staring at me with the eye it has left. "Fuck you, manatee," I mutter and kick off the sandals. There are band-aids over the stitches and they come out tomorrow anyway, it'll be fine. The leftover shadows are shortening.

Max and Eddie aren't out front; stepping into the dark of the cave my eyes adjust enough to see two silhouettes at the back. Not sure of my boundaries, I lean against the fender. Looking into the open cavity of the car, the cement below is visible.

"Bridget!"

Can't see his face, but the delight sounds genuine.

"Hey Max – stopped to see Maggie."

"You make friends with everybody, everywhere you go?" Teasing voice. The closer his outline gets the higher my stomach climbs.

"Yes. I enjoy asking inappropriate questions to strangers until they're left with no choice but to be my friends." I look up into his face – in the dimness he's less shy of eye contact. With one step I close the distance to within a foot. "You're tall."

Dark t-shirt, a little dirty but not filthy. His eyes are black marbles; in here the sun only hits sharp angles and bright things – eyes, knuckles, a jar of coins on a shelf, random bits of glass.

He sighs a sigh I do not understand.

"Bridget, what happened to your shoes?" Eddie approaches, nerve-endings all on the outside.

"You wore shoes?"

"Eh, stitches, it's stupid – forget it, Eddie, I ditched em." Pushing loose hair behind my ears, I don't look at either of them.

"Are they *your* shoes?" Eddie asks. I'm the goat today, the scapegoat.

"No, they're Charlotte's – oh you're right. I'll -"

Max laughs. "Sit down, Eddie'll get em. Right?"

"Of course. Be right back." Eye daggers at me.

The garage opens into a junky living room layout once we edge past the car. A couple stools and an old armchair, a fridge with a greasy black handle – indications of more. For height, I choose a stool. Max falls into the armchair; I'm satisfied with the illusion of power. Close enough to look up my skirt, he unfolds his hand. "Let's see the stitches."

"Already? I was hoping for a little foreplay." My laugh cracks and I snake my leg through the air.

"You that far in, that fast?" Leaving out the smile, he looks into my face. Impossible to read his.

It's so perfectly calculated. This is the place for shady deals and nervous agreements. Tension and lying, pressure and feigned confidence – the light is designed for these things.

A pause threatens, like a hand over my lungs. "Yeah," I answer, "I think I am." Cocking my head in the direction of his gutted project, I thrust my foot into his hand. "That was a very non-coy thing to ask."

"Mmmm, it's easy to be truthful when no one can see your eyes." Max's palm slips under my heel and he bracelets my ankle. "It's also easy to lie." Turning it by degrees, the angle nearly painful, he pulls up the Barbie band-aids from one side to see the thread. "I have shoes for you, I didn't forget."

"I know."

"This hurt?"

"Not in a way I'm gonna tell you to stop – oh you mean the – no, not really..." I tilt on the stool. "I don't know how to play how you people play. Never occurred to me it was a skill I needed to pick up."

"It's not." Max presses the band-aids back into place with his thumb and leans back. "It's all about getting around it."

"Like the dark back here?" Spinning my ankle, a tingling ache, I curl and uncurl my toes.

Eddie's phone announces his entrance, and Max clears his throat. So much can be expressed in a simple noise - now I know Max is annoyed with Eddie.

"Just be a second," Eddie is a construction paper cut-out with the sun burning behind him; Max becomes afterimages when I turn back.

Leaning as far forward as I dare, I whisper, "Are you enjoying this?"

"This?" He pinches one of my toes with scrubbed, stained fingers. "Probably as much as you. That?" Gesturing to Eddie. "Not one bit." His face is yellow in match flame, he hands the cigarette to me and lights another. "Your friend is very dramatic and very..." dragging on the cigarette, thinking. "Slippery."

"He's not my friend," I smile.

"Interesting."

Not having seen many noir films, the sense of black and white and mystery falls over us all the same. Maybe it's the cigarette smoke, or that I unknowingly crossed my legs.

Temple on his fist, elbow on the chair's worn arm, Max says, "I predict that Eddie will leave within the next ten minutes. I'm gonna make you stay with me, but don't be scared. He will be. But it's just a game – if he doesn't leave you here he won't come back today, and I need him to come back."

"Would you have me stay anyway?"

"I don't know."

"I'm not fucking with you on purpose." I flick ashes onto the floor, my mouth turned downward.

"I know," Max nods. "But it's...doing both at once. You don't lie, so I keep telling the truth, and that's a bad habit." He drops his cigarette into a grimy coffee can.

"You boys act like you're in the movies."

"It's all a bit small-time for that," Max laughs. "But you're partially right. I mean, I get a pretty hostage for a guaranteed delivery."

"So... Eddie's like a mule?" Trying on his squint, in here where he can't see.

"How am I supposed to intimidate your boyfriend if I'm laughing? In reality he's a very inefficient UPS man, and I'm like a UPS station."

"A very efficient UPS station?" Incredible that I can still blow smoke rings. Flicking the butt into the same can he did, I cross my legs the other way.

"Yes, I'm a very efficient UPS station, and I don't want things to get muddled, or – we've gone far enough with the UPS thing, right? You get that I'm pissed and he's fucking up."

"Not exactly why you're telling me, but yeah, I get it."

"Because I have to scare him a little, to speed him up, but I don't want to scare *you*. This is just part of the movie shit, alright?" Rushing through the last part as Eddie approaches, Max leans back in his chair.

Whatever. This is a lot like a movie.

Eddie's hands are jammed in his pockets. "Could we talk a minute?"

Without moving, Max answers, "Sure."

"Outside, maybe?"

"Hey whatever you have to say to him you can say to me." This is fun - Max hides a grin with his hand, turning it into a thinking, mouth-stroking motion.

"Bridget." But Eddie's dirty looks are powerless here.

"We'll be right back," My hand shoots out involuntarily as Max follows Eddie, almost touching his abdomen, but I draw back at the last second and fold my hands on my knees.

Like watching shadow puppets. The rectangular doorframe cuts the scenery into a television screen, or a stage with open curtains. The interior of the garage is real, but on the screen the volume is muted or the microphones are faulty or something. In the space of two minutes they return and I'm almost blind.

"…under two hours," Eddie finishes, and I keep my hands to myself as they pass.

"We'll be here."

"Okay, cool, I – what?" Eddie pushes the sandals at me and looks sideways at Max. "Bridget, let's go."

"No, it's fine. She can hang out here – no reason to drag her around with you. We'll be waiting right here for you." I can almost see horns on Max as he sinks deep into the armchair. An arousing optical illusion. "Fine with you, right, Bridget?" His voice is not quite the same one from two minutes ago.

Shrugging, "I don't care."

Eddie taps his foot, holding Charlotte's sandals with

both hands. His brain is transparent: It's one thing to pick me up from a mental facility, drag me around on various criminal activities, have sex with me – but leave me with someone who obviously scares him a little?

To be perfectly honest I'm a bit touched by this evidence of conscience.

"Bridget, come here for a second, okay? We'll be right back," he reassures Max. At the front fender he stops. "Are you okay with this?" Eddie whispers.

"Why wouldn't I be?"

"Look, I tried to tell you, he's not who you think –"

"Eddie, I'm not scared of him," I smile, feeling the sun on my face. "Do what you have to do, and don't by any means rush because of me."

Shoving the sandals into my hands, he grits his teeth. "Fine. Don't piss him off – and don't fuck him."

"Bye Eddie."

He backs away. "Back soon," he calls to Max. The El Camino sputters to life; I lean against the fender until the rumble is far away.

"What did he say?" Max close behind me.

"Not to fuck you."

With a laugh, I hear him retreat. "You're right, you're not his girlfriend."

"People focus their entire beings almost every moment behaving properly and not touching - Oh my god I just said that out loud."

Max pauses, leaning against one of the workbenches

along the walls.

"I thought I was just thinking it."

"You do that a lot?"

"No. Just when I'm tired." I drop into his armchair and put my bare feet up on the stool. Lighting a cigarette from his pack, I lean back and smile. "Crazy."

"It's a nice crazy."

A little time inside and your eyes adjust; that's the trick.

Max wears an almost naked look. He puts his right palm flat on the top of my right foot and runs it along the bone, up to the knee. "Eddie's jumpy when he's here. You're not afraid at all?" He lowers himself, folds his hand over my kneecap.

"Why would I be? What's the worst you could have done, the worst you can do? I don't care. I think you're fucking beautiful. It's wearing me out trying to say the right things." With one finger I trace his eyebrow. "Lying is exhausting."

"We're exact opposites." He leans forward, taking my cigarette with careful fingers.

"No we're not. You're perfectly honest about being a liar. Why don't you kiss me?"

"Because I don't want to." Max reads from a cue card that materialized behind me.

"Tell me better lies or tell me the truth." Taking the cigarette back, my insides pull against gravity, towards him, but not strong enough to lift my body.

"Because I want to." He watches his own hands.

Placing them on my collarbones, Max's thumbs slide along my shoulders, burning warm welts into my skin. He closes his hands around my upper arms, hard. "Why doesn't your face change when I do that?" Yanking me forward, close.

"You won't hurt me."

Letting go, Max stands and I fall back into the chair.

"It's not gonna happen, Bridget."

"Yes it is." I toss the cigarette. Looking up at him, "I thought about you all week. And we only met for ten minutes - that's pretty fucking scary. It can't get any scarier than that. Being back is easier than waiting to come back."

"You *waited* to come back?"

"Yes."

"Why didn't you just come back?"

Deep breath, I knot my fingers and look down. "Because it doesn't work that way. Because – you said Tuesday."

"You're a bad liar."

"It's a symptom of being too honest."

He turns away, manipulating something with a tool I don't recognize.

"You're going to get your hands dirty."

"They're already dirty."

"No they're not. Not today. You knew Eddie was a fuck-up and would leave, you knew you would keep me here. Is that as far as you thought it through?" I stand. Can't swallow, afraid my throat will click and he'll hear it.

"Yes." Quiet, back still to me. "You make it sound a lot more…. orchestrated than it was, but that's about right." The broken pieces clink as he tosses them and turns. His eyes are cold, bottomless. "I wasn't sure exactly how it would play out, but I'd planned my afternoon around fucking you, yeah."

Everything goes rubber when he says 'fucking' – all the backbone of the chair is gone. It's just me, and he is very tall. I hear myself ask, "So what are you waiting for?"

The dust motes freeze in the shafts of sunlight, the air in my lungs is the last I can find. A sliver of light from the bathroom doorway falls across his folded arms and the dead radio at his hip. My lungs open; I smell oil and gasoline and him.

Desperate, I put up both hands, flat against the thin air between us. "Just kiss me."

The space disappears and his hands grip my upper arms, pressing to my bones, my open palms against his shirt front - but he's not like flesh through the cotton, it's the same sense of touching a statue as when I first shook his hand. I have the chance to blink once, his eyes are black; my mouth burns when he presses his to it. No breath, no gravity, just a soft burn that bleeds from his lips and tongue into mine, and down the front of me in every place our bodies meet. I will not crash to the floor - magnets in my insides hold me to him, upright. My fingers just begin to curl, begin to search for purchase, for any yield in him, when he pushes me back – the force of coming apart almost audible, like tearing fabric. I hear it in my head, and the burn disappears, the fire on my tongue dissolving.

He shoves me away. Close to tumbling over, I finally understand what there is to fear: He lacks hesitation. It is almost inhuman.

Max is backed against the bench again, arms folded same as before.

Without the ache in my arms I might not believe it happened. "It's not fair anyone else in the world gets to touch you."

"I could say the same about you," he spits back, swatting my hand away when I reach out.

Pushing roughly past me, he falls into his chair, lighting a cigarette and passing it to me like before. I climb onto the stool. The clocks wind back, there is a sense of dream falling over the whole place - film noir. "I changed my mind. You'd fuck everything up." Max widens his eyes, opens his palms. "You know I'm telling you the truth. There wouldn't be any bending you over the car and pounding you and sending you home. Is that what you want? Because that's all I've got room for."

"Why?" I exhale, feeling very much like the caterpillar in Alice in Wonderland. "I only ask for one day a week. This..." I wave my hand between us, "it's too good to waste."

"One day a week. What the fuck does that mean?"

"Why do you want everything to stay the same?"

"Same reason you do."

"And why is that?"

"Because I understand things the way they are now, and I have everything in order – yeah, I told you I had you figured out." Max gives me that cat grin, the cat with feathers in his claws. "You walked in last week with Eddie and I knew you."

"So we aren't opposites."

"I know exactly what I'm doing – and that's the way I need it to be."

"But it's already happened." I laugh. "It's already fucked everything up for both of us. But it's okay." I lunge at him, my lips are against his before he can push me away – he tries, but the burn sets in. The grip that left bruises on my arms digs into my hips, he drags me forward onto his lap. Max gathers my hair in his hand, and sinks his teeth into my shoulder.

The almost-scream jars him.

He makes the human translation of a growl as he removes his mouth from my skin, the vibration runs to the tips of my toes.

"No, don't stop!" I can't breathe and everything aches; I am pissed and I am in love. He unwinds my hands from his neck and shoves me hard; like a doll I tumble into the chair.

Almost immediately the ache settles in, deep, everywhere he touched me. "You're a monster," I smile at him. "It's wonderful."

"Listen Bridget, I don't –"

"But you do!"

"I'm not doing this, and you're not doing this, so just sit your ass in the chair and stop."

"Control, yes, I get it." Pouting is not a word I am particularly fond of, but I curl up, chin on knees, hands around my ankles, and no matter how much he glows I will not look at him.

The sparks in the air are disappearing. "Why does everyone in your world only want things they can control? And to only feel safe things? Anything that's more than a tiny blip on the heart monitor and you freak the fuck out."

"My world, you say." Max gets two Cokes from the fridge and hands one to me. Holding it with the tips of my fingers I stretch, knowing if I drop it the glass will shatter. Before it can happen I draw my arm back in.

A silence settles; as usual my anger melts. No one ever compares anger to hot wax, but they should. It's fluid and easily shed; it cools quickly and flakes off, leaving no trace.

"Eddie doesn't deserve to put his hands on you."

"What's the difference?"

Max's hair is a bit disheveled after the battle, sexier. He's squinting again, smoking again, he leans back in the folding chair with a heel on his ankle. "When you said you were crazy you weren't all the way joking, were you?"

"Not all the way, no. There may be some paperwork somewhere or something," I mutter; I don't like where this has gone. "What does it matter? You don't want me. You say not to let Eddie touch me. That's fucking ridiculous."

"That was advice."

"It sounded like an order."

"I'm used to talking that way."

"That how you talk to your skanky girlfriend with the bleachy hair and stupid shoes?" Uncurling, I place the Coke bottle gently next to the chair.

"Don't get a word in edgewise most of the time."

"She got lots of important things to talk about?"

"Couldn't say." Max grins. "I'm not much of a listener."

"Yes you are. Why you with her, then? What's she got that I don't?" Folding my own arms in a challenge, I raise my eyebrows, trying on one of Amy's tough-girl faces. "What's she got at all?"

Max sighs, tired as me. "Jesus, Bridget, I'm almost forty years old and I'm used to her. She gives a hell of a blow job and never asks for anything more complicated than jewelry. We've been together awhile, she doesn't want to move in or get married – she just likes having a shady boyfriend that buys her pretty stuff." He leans forward. "She's a lot like Eddie."

"Eddie never wants me to buy him things."

"She's simple. I never have to think about her."

I blink. "I don't think you heard what you just said."

His cigarette sails through the air into the coffee can. "I did. I think we should stop talking."

"I think we should have sex."

"Bridget."

"Max." I press my head against the chair. "It hurts to think of her hands on you. Why did you say that about her, about blow jobs? I can't know that." Curling my legs under me, I keep my eyes on him.

"Don't look so mad. Damnit, I could really hate you for this mess."

A rumble of cars approaching, Max lifts his eyebrows and turns his head. He looks tired and keyed-up simultaneously, it only takes a second to figure out he's relieved to find a new place to direct his adrenaline. "Come on, I'll take you upstairs." He stands with a groan, the muscles in his forearms twisting beneath his skin.

Reaching for him, both arms out, I am only half-surprised when he slides his arms under my knees and shoulders. My face pressed into his neck, I don't see the stairs to the apartment, just hear his boots. The curtains are pulled shut; raising my head, my brain is too full to devour and make sense of the outlines of furniture.

Max eases me onto an unmade twin bed. His arms disappear, but he stands over me a moment. His every environment is designed to disguise what he's thinking.

"If you're trying to decide what to do, the answer is climb on," I smile, voice flat and tired even to me.

Shaking his head, "Just looking."

"What are you going to do?"

"None of your goddamned business," he smiles. "Stay here."

His boots are loud on the stairs. The pillow smells like exhaustion and fabric softener and I press my face into it.

An unfamiliar laugh may be the most horrifying thing to hear in an unfamiliar place. It adds doom to disorientation.

There is a bookshelf with spines all facing in, the books in stacks instead of rows - I've spent the last fifteen minutes studying the ones I can reach from the bed, careful to replace each one exactly the way I found it. I'm warm with the imprint of unfamiliar sheets, but I hear the strange laugh again.

Pressing my hands to sore hipbones assures me none of this was imagined. I tiptoe to the open door.

I creep down a few steps to listen. The conversation is in another language – one involving money, scheduling, phone calls, and terms about electronics. Easier to focus on the voices; I cover my mouth with both hands to insure silence.

There are three. The laughing voice is nervous; the laughter is a defense, it's I'm-not-sure-my-statements-are-satisfactory punctuation. There is a quiet angry voice, whose words would be indistinguishable even if I tried. And there is Max - but not. Not the same Max, I mean. I heard a hint of this when he told Eddie he would keep me, monotone and matter of fact. But this is the voice of Cold Max, and the other voices have no choice but to listen.

This phenomena is extraordinary – like when a girl Sandra nicknamed Sybil lived at the home for about three weeks. She had different voices for different facial expressions – for a little while we had a blast, betting which voice would come out based on facial expression, then approaching to strike up a conversation. Sybil stabbed Gerald in the crotch with a plastic fork at lunch time during one of these experiments, and she disappeared. Gerald blamed himself for baiting her, but I had guessed she was wearing her bitch face before he walked over.

The stairs are tempting; I want to see what Cold Max looks like. He's been the only one speaking for at least the last sixty seconds. One bare foot in front of the other I think "stealthy, stealthy" and try to slink.

I manage to get three more stairs behind me and can see into the garage now, recognizing Max by his extra-messed hair. His shoulders are broader and the relaxed cat is gone from him – they resemble three wary dogs, Max with the most intimidating posture. Slowly the others are accepting this - the quiet angry dog is relaxing his arms and neck as he listens.

The things he's saying make no sense to me, things about bad blood, the word business. Max changes focus from the quiet angry dog to the dog with the nervous laugh and says more things, I can't focus on the words. He trails off, spotting me at the top of the stairs, his eyes are black and blank - for a moment there is absolutely nothing behind them. He blinks, beginning to come back, and the pause is long enough to make the others turn.

Quiet Angry smiles. "Oh, my sister is going to love this."

Cold Max reappears, snapping his head back around. "You didn't even see her. Nothing that goes on in here is any of your fucking business unless I say it is. You want this to stay professional? Focus on your watch." Max lights a cigarette; with adjusted eyesight I see Quiet Angry's shocked eyebrows. "There are plenty of guys with better time-telling skills than you without gold-digging sisters." With dead eyes he looks up at me, pointing with his cigarette. "Get your ass back upstairs. This's got nothing to do with you."

Not sure whether to clap or wet myself, I run back up, slamming the door so it sounds as if I were inside the apartment. Hands back over my mouth on the top step, I hear Quiet Angry dissolve into Calm Reassurance. I can make out Max's words; the tone means more, but his voice carries.

"Straighten this out by Monday and we call it even. Otherwise fuck you and your sister."

My heart thumps through the closing conversation and the sounds of car doors and a retreating engine. Footsteps on the stairs, Max looks up to see me pressed against the door. Coming back behind the eyes, relaxing around the mouth, he tries to explain. "You know that was bullshit, right? That was playing."

"I get it."

"I didn't mean to scare you."

"You didn't." Smiling, I lower myself to the top step, sitting in the doorway to rush being eye to eye as he ascends. "It's very exciting, you're two different people. And like forty versions of in-between."

He opens his mouth, but instead of speaking, reaches above my head and I hear the doorknob, feel the door slide from behind me. Placing one palm between my breasts and pushing me down, my shoulders flat on the carpet, Max covers my mouth with his. There's a sizzle, the crackle of fusing in my head, and my dress is around my waist and his belt is cold in my hands, clattering, the zipper loud, his boots grind on the steps and with one intake of breath, I take one large pull of oxygen from his own lungs, he's inside me, and it burns, burns like thrusting your palms toward the fire when they're ice cold, burns like being Not

Empty and maybe he's the one that's cold and I'm hot inside, and I can't see him, only taste and feel and shudder and he's heavy on top of me with my hands in the small of his back, slick muscles, and he pushes harder and breathes again into my mouth, my insides wrap into electric hands, squeezing blue light, I push my hips upward and bite down into his lip, he slides his hand under me and exhales once more, a growl and a push with his digging fingertips, and I taste his blood in my mouth before he breaks the kiss and falls against me, onto me, his cheek against mine, fingers tangled, my knees sliding down the sides of his jeans, the seams searing my skin, shaky, my bare feet coming to rest beside his boots.

We stay this way. I link my fingers under his shirt behind his back, and he slides his hands under my head, weight on his elbows. I can see all the way back now, all the way to the back of his skull. His black eyelashes frame windows.

This is what sex is supposed to be like.

"You said that out loud." He smiles, almost. "Your mouth is all bloody."

"It's your blood." He's still inside me. "Stay like this. Stay where you are. I'm afraid it'll be broken if you're not inside me."

"My dick?"

I smile a bloody smile. "The spell."

His hair is everywhere, mine is under his elbows. He sighs. "This is not what it's supposed to be like."

"Yes it is," I whisper. "It's just not what it's *usually* like."

Max stares. "Is Bridget your real name?"

"No."

"Does everyone call you Bridget, or is it something you made up when you came here?"

"Everyone. Not just you."

"Does Eddie know your real name?"

"No."

"Were you really roommates with his sister?"

"Yes, his twin sister. And yes, I was sleeping with her, too."

"Where is she?"

"Six feet under."

"For how long?"

"Almost two years."

"How old are you?"

"Twenty-seven. Everyone thinks I'm twenty-four."

"Everyone as in your friends?"

"Yes, and Eddie."

"Your friends in..."

"Neverland. The place where I live. Do you really want to know more?"

"I haven't decided."

"It's safer for people if I don't live...outside. But I could probably leave if I wanted. Does that make sense?"

"Not really."

"Think of where I live...think of it like an orphanage

instead of jail. Maybe at some point the people where I'm from were dangerous, or troublesome, but now they just have nowhere else to be, or no one to take care of them. Like orphans. So we stay there, like in a dream, or an island. Like Lost Boys."

"Have you always been there?"

I laugh. I can feel him inside me, the laugh making him hard again. "Since when has anyone always been anywhere?"

"You can leave whenever you want?"

"Not exactly."

"Do you want to leave?"

"Sometimes. It's better I don't. Things are better for other people if I'm there."

"What does that mean?" Max moves, just a little, just enough.

"I - I hurt people sometimes."

"Physically?"

"Sometimes."

"Anyone I know?"

"Yes."

"Have you killed anyone?"

"That's something I could ask you. Take me to the bed."

"Would it matter if I had?" He asks, and moves again, my words aren't going to work much longer.

"No. Would it matter if I had?"

One hand sliding to my hip, he pushes, deep, deep, then finally Deep Enough, and I wind my legs around him. "I can't see how it would matter," he whispers.

"My friend Gerald says we're broken birds, in a gilded cage."

"You don't feel broken."

The afternoon passes in the twin bed, and it's good that Eddie is a liar, that his two hour promise means nothing.

There's little talking, glass bottles of Coke from the fridge, a box of powdered donuts. Max has a tattoo of a ship, larger than my hand, on his right shoulder blade. Two inch-wide scars above his left hipbone, shiny white. I imagine all I need to know of his past, my thighs against the scars, him beneath me. I ask him nothing.

Only when the sun starts to really slide, when it's getting orange outside the blinds, leaving bloody stripes on the sheets, on my arm across his chest, does Max tell me I have to get dressed. "It's almost six."

I pull my dress over my head, my panties are long gone. "What happens now?"

In the evening light, he remembers himself, remembers The World. His face is changing back. I watch him put on his human skin with his jeans. "I don't know."

The spell is broken.

"What's your real name?" Max asks from the door.

His eyes are soft, but his eyebrows are finding their scowl. He finger-combs his hair back.

Looking at the floor, at my bare feet, I answer, "I'll tell you next time."

He frowns, but the old phone below proves it is indeed functional by trilling like a bird.

I follow him downstairs and curl up in his chair while he talks, his back to me.

"Bridget?" Cautious, small voice.

I hop up to peer over the car. "Maggie!"

Max glances over his shoulder, surprised by the little girl in the doorway, but turns back to his conversation.

Skirting the car, I see her in silhouette – her feet flush against each other, nervous to be here.

"Hey Bridget. Is Max back there?"

"He's on the phone. It's okay you're here, he's secretly really nice only don't tell anybody I said so, especially not him."

Lifting her eyebrows, she looks around me, checking to see if we're talking about the same person. Satisfied, she thrusts an arm out. "This is for Sandra. Only for her to open. I have to go now. Will you be back sometime? Are you Max's girlfriend now?" Dancing her way back down the concrete ramp.

I can only shrug. "We'll see."

Everything is ending abruptly. Eddie's El Camino in sight, Maggie runs away waving, her flip-flops slapping and throwing gravel.

Before the El Camino parks I run back inside and put my arms around Max, cheek to his back. Like hugging a stone until he takes a deep breath; he covers both my hands with his free one. Slamming the phone onto its hook and turning, he breaks my grip. "Is that Eddie?"

The engine cuts out.

I nod and Max puts his hand on the back of my neck, sliding it under my hair and squeezing. His face is a jumble, sliding in and out of different masks. "Go out front, I have to talk to him by myself." He rubs his palm across the red mark on my shoulder, waking up the bruise from his teeth, and frowns. "Don't let him touch you, okay? Please. Please, no more Eddie. Go."

"Do you want me to come back?"

"I have to think." His eyes are sad and a little tired; I don't like it. Trying to loop my arms around him, he grabs my wrists and pushes me back. "Bridget, go."

Every place he touched tingles, and nothing is finished. We are only three sentences into every conversation and it's over. Maggie's envelope in one hand and Charlotte's sandals in the other, I walk away without looking at him again.

"Hey Bridget, are you okay?"

"Fuck you, Eddie." I push past him without looking up, and break into a run.

The El Camino smells like old onion rings but I'm used to it. I circle myself with my arms, my throat closes before I realize what is happening. I'm going to cry.

Staring at the stupid manatee, both hands pressed to my chest, I will the tightness away. Two years since I cried, and if it ever happens again it will not be for something like this. Not for a person. I will not cry.

The evening ride drips quiet. The thing is, Eddie is relaxed; whatever trouble he was in has been resolved - but next to him is me, a silent and bruise-covered Eeyore.

He rides the conscience fence again. Looking into his skull, I think Eddie secretly believes whatever Max and I did while he was gone put him back in good graces. So, Eddie's enormous self-centeredness is having a tiny battle with an under-developed concern for others, which lucky for him will last only until I am out of the car and he no longer sees the fingerprints on my arms.

My heart slid down my insides, past my broken clockwork pieces and between my legs to hit the concrete with a bloody splat when Max said "Go". Nothing else, just Go. It's lying there now in the half-light in front of his arm chair, like the mouse an alley cat would drag in as the best she had to offer. After he steps on it, his boots will track it all over the concrete to mix with the stains and other footsteps – Max will be walking on me for years.

We pull into the Sex Park, the drive-thru totally skipped. I try to think of what word Gerald would use and come up with both 'incredulous' and 'indignant'.

"Did he hurt you?"

"Yes."

"Like bad?"

"Yes. Why are we here?"

Eddie spreads his hands in defense as a gang of ducks waddles in front of the car. "Just to talk, Bridget. I'm not gonna touch you."

"Because he told you not to?"

Silence, which is the same as Yes. Well, not true. Silence is usually the answer the other person thinks you don't want to hear. Taking Max's cigarettes from the breast pocket of my dress – Sandra makes them flat-fronted with a middle pocket, like the kind dolls wear – I light one with stolen matches and shake my head. "You're incredible, you know that, Eddie?" The ducks turn to stalk past the car again and I flash them a Wu Tang W, smiling.

His fingers drum the steering wheel, eyes on the cigarettes and book of matches. "Okay. So – okay. Maybe something was said…" Eddie stares across the lake – like he can't even see the ducks. "He hurt you bad?"

"Yes Eddie, he hurt me bad. Bad like fuck off and stop asking me. I know you straightened your shit out, I can see it in your face." Smoke gathered; I crank down the window and the last of my composure floats out with it.

"If you go to the doctor when I take you home, you have to make sure and tell them I didn't-"

"Jesus Christ, Eddie!" My voice is louder than either of us expect. "Do you really think he's like that? Do you think I am? You seriously think a guy you work with or for or whatever fucked me back into being cool with you, and the most you have to say about it is to tell the doctors it wasn't you that did the damage? What the fuck is wrong with you?" I twist the cigarette into the back of his white-knuckled hand.

Eddie screams first and backhands second. The slap lacks a good wind-up and does little more than make him scream again when his raw skin hits my cheek. "You fucking bitch!" He cradles his hand, grimacing. "What am I supposed to think? You run to the car when I get there - and he tells me we're cool, but if I so much as try to hold your hand he'll break my fucking fingers."

"He said that? He said he'd break your fingers?"

"I will admit I am – selfish. Shit, I just wanna get work, Bridget. It's not like I'm a bad guy. But Max is a monster."

"True."

"I knew you were going to fuck him when I left – you same as told me! I tried to warn you." He pokes at the blistering spot on his hand and takes a huge breath. "Was it bad enough that you won't go back? If he asked me to bring you? I could give a shit what you think of me, just answer."

"What?" The ducks scatter as a truck sans muffler pulls in beside us. I rub the matchbook with both thumbs – it reads "Tuesday's Bar & Grill" in gold letters and there are only five left – and my stomach dares to stir, just a little. "He – what? You think he wants…" I can barely hear myself, but that's no gauge of volume.

"Fuck if I know. But he was serious about the – the hands-off thing. I just thought – shit, I don't know. Would you? If he asked for you, would you go back?"

Never having heard talk like this – me addressed as pretty much a negotiable commodity – makes me want to jam another lit cigarette into Eddie, but I don't care what Eddie thinks. I can feel the anger dissipate, float away. Striking another match, I exhale the last of my rage with the smoke from Max's cigarette.

My heart lies on the greasy floor of a garage.

Just a little bit of hope. A twinkle of possibility. Just enough to make the cigarette taste better, and the envelope for Sandra important again – just enough to turn "Go" into "Go – for now".

"Of course I'll go back." I rub my shoulder with my palm, the way Max did. "I did fuck him, and I would again, you were right. I think I'm in love with him, Eddie."

"You crazy bitch."

"Take me home. Nothing you say right now can upset me. Just tell me what he wants – whatever he wants. I'll do whatever he wants."

Eddie's twitchy; it's after dark so he has to drive me all the way to the house and sign me in. They buzz the gate and it swings open wide, slow. I'm digging in the backseat of his car.

"If you're looking for the shoebox, I've got it. He told me to make sure you got it."

The shoes. I'd forgotten. I run my tongue along my swollen lips, rummaging until I come up with a purple sweater. It smells like gardenia perfume and onion rings.

"You can't take that, it's my girlfriend's."

"Fuck your girlfriend," the sweater is too big, but cloaks all the fingerprint bruises, all the teeth marks.

"Yvonne works the desk nights, you remember Yvonne? So it's the sweater or you explain why I look like I fell down some stairs."

The light from the house slides on and off his face, his lips make a tight line, like doll's lips, stitched into resigned silence. Eddie pushes a plain white shoebox at me, then Charlotte's sandals. I slip them on as he yanks the El Camino's parking brake at the bottom of the steps.

"Late night!" Yvonne whistles, and her brown eyes slide up and down Eddie in disapproval. Sandy may be Mom, but Yvonne is Grandma. "Evening, Mr. Helm."

"Evening, Mrs. Hayes."

"You have a good day, darling? Stephen said he saw you last week."

I shake my head and smile, dismissing her implied inquiry -Stephen is Barney's real name- and sign the book in the column next to Eddie's in the row next to 9:30pm. "Tuesdays are the best days. Not necessarily because of this one here," I cock my head at Eddie and she laughs. He shuffles. "But nothing beats the lake on a sunny day. Time got away from us I guess."

"You're fine, darlin'. Missed Sandy and Charlotte by just a few minutes - say, Eddie! Will you be here for the Fourth of July dinner? I know your aunt will be. I'm sure she'd appreciate your presence."

"I - I hadn't thought about it." There are light bulbs exploding above his head, sucking the color from his face. "Mrs. Hayes, could I talk to Bridget for just one more second?"

Her lids drop. "As long as it's inside these doors."

She asks me about the shoebox, and the envelope, and the cigarettes.

I tell her the envelope's not mine, and I'm sorry about the cigarettes, and as for the shoebox, "I'm not supposed to see 'til tomorrow, don't show me."

I spin away, Charlotte's sandals clacking, but not before I see her smile as she lifts the lid.

"What did you tell Max about me?" He hisses.

"Nothing," I whisper. "You think we spent the day talking about *you*? Don't worry, Mr. Helm," I wink. "Now say a polite goodbye to Yvonne and get the fuck out of here. Tell your girlfriend thanks for the sweater."

When he's gone I turn to Yvonne, slipping off the sandals. "Do you like Charlotte? I was thinking of putting in to have her assigned as my roommate."

Yvonne beams. "You are really moving on. I was worried after last week, and I worry you hanging around..." she juts her chin at the door, at Eddie, "but I think you're just fine. And between you, me and the desk, that little girl's gonna be here awhile. Needs someone to show her *she's* going to be fine. Stephen says she talks in her sleep to her mother about the piano every time she's - well, you know." Yvonne predates HIPAA. And her nephew tells her everything.

We are, after all, a family.

I don't look in the box Max sent, just stack the Shoebox - retrieved from beneath the sign over my doorway, purple marker on yellow construction paper, "Magic is Play" - on top of it and push them both under the bed. I don't cry in the shower, most of Max can't be washed off me. He turned my skin into a rainbow.

Working a comb through my lavender-stinking wet hair, the mirror fog fades and I see flesh tone in the sink on the opposite wall. My knees shake just a little and I lose hold of the comb.

Tiptoeing to the opposite sink, my pajama pants shushing me along on the tiles, I know what I'll see before I see it.

Emma, facedown and naked, floating in a sink that's been plugged with paper towels.

"Shit."

Turns out it's not my voice, but Charlotte's, from the doorway. Her eyes are round, lips going white.

I put a finger to my lips - Ssshhh - and reach under the doll, digging loose the makeshift plug. "Help me squeeze the water out."

We hold the doll upside down, twisting her in unspeakable ways, but manage to mostly empty her. I wrap her in my towel and Charlotte follows me to my room. We go to work on the gooey, half-peeled band-aids.

We sit for a few minutes in silence on the blue-flowered bedspread, working over the doll with combs and fingernails, and it's sort of nice to have someone in the room that isn't personnel. Long time since Mandy Lynn bit the dust, and though no one blames me, they're a bit superstitious. There are at least five of the forty or so coherent residents that will tell you I never should have planted that painted doll, but a Barbie dipped in acrylic didn't kill her. Mandy Lynn was one-minded, she never varied in her only wish. It was just a matter of opportunity and Eddie.

"Why don't you have anything on the walls?"

"What?"

Charlotte sweeps her arm through the air. "Pictures or anything. I – I mean not to… I just figured your room would be different…"

"I keep everything down there," I nod at the plot of soil, the strong necks bobbing in the wind. "Keeping stuff freaks me out. Things that don't move, you know? Dead things. It's cool that people have stuff, you know, that means something to them, but I guess I don't really get it. I have a few things, but I'm not sure if they mean…" Blinking, it takes a moment to realize how much I've said.

"Amy said you were a robot."

"What?" I laugh.

"She said you were a robot – that sometimes she wondered if you were just programmed to be here among us and gather data – that you were the perfect lunatic, with no weaknesses or surprises." Confession breeds confession.

"Did you believe her?"

"Are you kidding?" Charlotte laughs. "That bitch is crazy."

She looks a little surprised when I dig her band-aids out of the Shoebox and open them, but joins me in making the doll look as much like it had before.

"So the plan is we never mention this, ever. And if it happens again, we don't mention it then."

"Okay."

"But I'm going to tell Yvonne, all the same, so her doctor knows, but we're never going to mention that, either."

"Okay."

We wrap the doll in a dry towel and Charlotte holds her breath at Sandra's open door as I creep in, placing Emma in the clothes basket where she's been sleeping, the envelope from Maggie on top.

"What was that?"

"Don't know. Card or something from the little girl she made the dress for."

"Bridget...."

I stop, and we face each other in the hallway. Her fingers are dancing against her thighs, hard to believe I didn't pick up on the piano thing.

"Did Eddie hit you? Like a lot?"

"Just once."

Footsteps echo around the corner.

"I'll explain tomorrow - get in your room before we're both in trouble. Night, Charlotte."

"Night, Bridget."

We run in different directions, and I dive onto the bed before I hear, "Charlotte! It's almost eleven. Lights out, dear."

I flip the lamp, and wait for the footsteps to pass my door.

Wide awake at dawn Wednesday morning, I pull out the Shoebox and sort my family's problems, spreading them like a tarot deck.

I think about Max's tattoo as I spread the offerings.

A ship - a pirate ship or merchant ship? Doesn't matter, ships go away, travel far, escape.

I unfold a page torn from Dr. Spock, its focus on purple crying.

The ship, sailing away, running away from your troubles, escape.

The half-used box of band-aids.

A departing ship. Age. Realization that your problems drag along behind like an anchor, anyway.

A sealed envelope addressed to a woman I know is dead, the lettering in Gerald's hand. The envelope is just folded parchment, through it I can make out "sober seven years now..."

Blue waves, simply drawn as a row of Golden Spirals. An un-anchored ship. The futility of running. Discarding the dream of pure immunity, of a clean slate.

A rubber band ball. Envelope stuffed with confetti. Pink and green friendship bracelet.

Standing your ground. Untangling, rebuilding,

recreating...

I know, I know, I'm telling my story, and Max's and Charlotte's, Gerald's, Sandra's, everyone's, as I sort through the box.

Everyone's story is pretty much the same.

"Who bit you?"

Bless Amy for not fucking around. I'm wearing one of Charlotte's t-shirts over my dress, but I planted and weeded in the garden for an hour in just my sundress before Sandra brought it to me, Emma in the sling like nothing happened, spilling over with joy at the crayoned Thank You card she clutched in her other hand. It said at the bottom, in careful letters, Write Back Soon.

"Guy named Max."

"The new one? Juliet?"

"Yep."

"Jesus, if you aren't having all the fun. I haven't been fucked at all in three years, much less fucked to bruises."

"Amy!" Sandra covers Emma's ears, but Amy and Charlotte both hide smiles.

"Oh don't pretend to be so worried, Sandy. She's glowing. More than you, even, with your new pen pal. Will you get to see him again?"

"Don't know. He knows about here," I twirl my finger in the air, encompassing the terrace, the house, the gate.

Gerald releases a breath, and though he doesn't look up, I know what it means: he's relieved.

"How's Emma getting on?"

I look sideways at Charlotte, but she's only human.

Sandy turns the doll's plastic face up, to catch the sun. "We had a rough go of it the last couple nights, I thought she was colicky, but we seem to be past the worst of it." She smiles into the doll's face. "I'll tell Maggie in my letter that she's doing fine."

"Best leave out the part about you carrying her around, she might think you're nuts."

Charlotte snorts and puts both hands over her mouth.

"Dammit , Amy! That's just about enough!" Sandy pounds her fist on the table and the Occupational Therapist raises her eyebrows.

"Sandra," Gerald's voice is a quiet warning.

"I'm just - I don't understand what's going on with her today."

I clear my throat and look at Amy. She's made nothing but hearts with her clay today, and somehow infected us, we're all making them. The table is littered with hearts. I remember what Amy's hearts mean, they don't happen very often.

She meets my eyes and quickly looks back down, tears one of the hearts in two and promptly reconstructs it as two smaller hearts. "Friday."

Sandra's eyes widen. Gerald puts a hand over one of Amy's, she yanks hers away.

"My mom's coming Friday." Charlotte whispers. "Or she's supposed to. I don't know. She was supposed to come last Friday and didn't."

Amy reaches across the table, hooks her index finger around Charlotte's thumb. "My daughter hasn't visited in a year. She's supposed to be here this week, too."

"Why don't they come?"

"Because they're bitches," Amy smiles when Charlotte's head jerks up. "We're trying to be better people, there's nothing more those bitches can ask of us."

"Those bitches," Charlotte smiles and shakes her head.

We all return to the hearts, making the pile larger and larger.

His voice is that of Cold Max. "What the fuck are you doing here, Bridget? I don't want any trouble, so just turn your skinny ass around and get the fuck out." There's the shuffle of boots and rustle of clothing, I picture him pulling up his jeans; the sound of his zipper slices through my belly like a serrated blade. Hand over the wound, I look up.

Max gleams, blue hair and slick stomach, his eyes hollows, fumbling with his pants. It's impossible to look into his eyes and see what he really means. Snatching his shirt, it catches the knob on the radio, filling the cave with *Pancho and Lefty*.

"No trouble. I just came for that." Pointing, but neither of us look in the direction of the bloody organ in front of the armchair.

I sit straight up out of the dream, put my palms over my mouth to make sure I'm making no real sound. It isn't yet dawn. There's no light, but there will be soon. My legs are shaky, my hands clammy on my mouth.

Three boxes under the bed, I line them up on the tangled sheets before I get dressed. Even if I wash the sweat off me, I should still have time to finish my business before sunrise.

Benny Hinn was important to my grandmother. Deep down she knew he was a charlatan. She'd point two crooked fingers, Pall Mall sticking up between them, at the stacks of letters he prayed over and ask, "How much money do you think is in those letters? Just those, just a days' worth?" and smile in bitter admiration. "Look at that hair." But all the same, he looked out at her from the false window, and told her he was there. That he was listening. That he cared, that he prayed for her. It made no difference that he was probably lying. If he was listening, God might be listening, when there was no one else left to do it. I didn't have the strength to listen, not then. The TV screen reflected off her glasses and all I could see were two silver heads, like Greek coins on her eyelids.

Gerald and I started the garden during Mandy Lynn's last year, when the schizophrenia was to the point that she wouldn't let me around her in the daytime. "Yvonne will make it happen," Gerald said, "we can ask."

Mandy Lynn started planning her death a year in advance, explaining it to me at night when she was lucid. "I'm thirty," she said, "it's only going to get worse. Same as it did for Mom and Gran. I don't want to be another generation of Crazy. Wandering in the walnut trees naked in the middle of the afternoon talking to myself, on my little plot of family Crazy Land. Why? Why would I want that?" She studied Egyptian mythology, but I was never sure if sure if it was lucid Mandy Lynn or crazy Mandy Lynn that made the lists of things she wanted to take with her.

Eddie was at the top of the list.

I wear the dress with the ribbons, the first dress Sandra made for me, the first dress she made here.

Yvonne is staring at me, Visitor's Day is her early day. "Bridget, what are you doing?"

"I need to get these in the ground before anyone else is up," I hold up the boxes. "They need to know I've done all I could before it's time for people to not show up."

The only thing I've kept of Mandy Lynn's is a pink angora sweater with pearly-white buttons. I wear it now over my dress, barefoot in the dirt, stabbing with the spade over and over beneath the asters.

I need to dig my way back to the present. Memories are tightening around my skull, tilting my head side to side. Is this what it means, *Heavy is the head that wears the crown?* Does the weight of the past, the burden, roost and fester in the jewels and the gold, poisoning the brain, weakening the spine?

I tried to explain to Mandy Lynn about the pockets, about the rabbit holes - that everything that Melville said was wrong, or at least a misinterpretation, he had taken the right idea and turned it into something out of proportion, as out of proportion as a man facing a whale. "They're everywhere, you're never trapped. You can always go in, even if some don't lead very far. Even if they don't lead to another reality, they lead out of this one." Ahab believed you could punch through, and use that hole to tear down the backdrops, the curtain, deconstruct the stage. I wasn't so sure. I knew that every zero, every letter O, every hole, every crack, could be stretched, was an opening. If you stared hard enough, the world around a knothole on a tree would reveal itself as flat, two-dimensional, fake, exposed once the opening to Somewhere Else was found. Inside some were tunnels, inside others just enough space to fit yourself. We were never cornered, never without options. And who knew? Maybe one of these days we'd stumble onto one that was a real door, like Alice going down a rabbit hole or through the mirror. Like the leaks Kilgore Trout talked about.

"You read too much," she'd grinned, and handed over the doll, dipped in red. "If I go to another universe, it's through the doors I make in my arms."

The birds begin to titter, but there's no sun yet. I take off the sweater and lay it carefully behind me in the grass. The hole I've made is huge, big enough to sit in at least, more than enough space for the things I've brought.

For six months she worked on him, and at some point I started working on him, too. He was innocent, then, without ambition, without need to be Bad. Mandy Lynn and I placed him between us and squeezed. Eddie finally came around to the idea that his twin was beyond saving.

And on a Visitor's Day, two summers ago, he smuggled in a little .22, like she'd asked, presumably to use on herself. She wore a blue cocktail dress, and I'd braided daisies into her hair. We dragged Eddie into the Arts and Crafts room, and Mandy Lynn passed the gun to me, eyes full of fire. "Hurry! Before you change your mind!" and opened up her veins. I swung the gun and fired twice, Eddie's shirt growing two red roses on the right shoulder. Behind him on the terrace, a handful of goldfinches took flight, flashing yellow like they'd burst from the bulletholes made in the glass. The twins fell away from each other, and I wrapped Mandy Lynn's fingers around the gun, just like she planned. "Call for help," she reminded, and smiled. Her teeth were red, the front of her dress was red. She was beautiful. I took her free hand, and screamed and screamed.

Obviously I'm not a very good shot.

The shoes are too important to keep, or look at. I press the box that Max meant for me into the hole. If we never see each other again, or if we do, I won't judge us on what he thinks would anchor me to the earth.

Around the box goes everything from the Shoebox, the sky is lightening. Maybe I am superstitious. I cover it all, quick as I can. When the first yellow sliver appears over my back shoulder, I sigh. Balling Mandy Lynn's sweater into a pillow, I stretch out in the dewy grass, feet in the soil, and light a cigarette with dirty fingers.

It's becoming Friday morning. And there's nowhere I'd rather be than morning.

Three people arrive on Visitor's Day, three people for a total of fifty residents. Like every Friday, we all look like we're going to church. It's a kindness, for everyone to dress up on Fridays and Tuesdays, whether they expect anyone to visit on Fridays or pick us up on Tuesdays. It's easier to camouflage our disappointment if we're not the only ones looking our best. The guard with the two day a week job sits in the "shack" halfway down the hill between the house and the gate with a stack of blue magazines.

I wasn't looking for Eddie or Max. Charlotte and Amy pretend they weren't looking for anyone, either.

This is the second Friday in a row I check at the office in the evening. Eddie hasn't called in a pass for Tuesday. Not that I would've been allowed to leave, I'm Restricted by Dr. Matthews due to the bruises. Any visitors have to see me on the premises for the time being. It doesn't bode well for my Juliet, or Rosalind.

Sandra, Charlotte and I stay on the front porch well past sunset. I braid asters into Charlotte's hair and wind the braid around her head like a crown. Sandra calls attention to the lightning bugs, and we all pay attention to them for the first night that summer. Charlotte thinks it's funny - "lightning bugs" she says, "we always said fireflies."

"Maybe they're fireflies out there," Sandra says with a small smile, and puts Emma to her shoulder, "but they're lightning bugs in here."

"You know, it's really not a bad life," Charlotte says. She turns to face me, and under the crown of flowers and hair, her eyebrows are high and her mouth open.

"It's okay," Sandra tells her. "I was surprised when I realized I didn't want to die, too."

Charlotte plucks at one of the band-aids with her teeth. Three left.

Tuesday morning, I'm pulling weeds, the sun is stroking my head and all is right with the world.

Since I buried the shoes, I only dream about water.

When the sun is high, and my shadow is short, I'm out of weeds. I push myself back on my heels in the cool dirt and turn my face up into the sun.

"Bridget!" It's an aide, calling from behind me.

"I didn't do it!" I call back, and stand, arching my spine. I make an ellipses, then a complimentary one, and two vertebrae pop like firecrackers.

"Eddie Helm's down at the gate. He can't take you out, but you can walk down to talk to him."

"He can't even come in the gate?"

"Brought an unauthorized male with him. Shane's in the guard shack, he'll keep an eye on y'all."

"Goddamnit, Kelly, I know you're from Washington, quit with the y'all business." I'm not nervous, not going to be nervous. It's Max, I know it's Max.

"Watch your mouth, Bridget. You going? I'll call down to Shane."

"Yeah, I'm going."

Sandra's beside me, stroller and all, before I can blink. "I'm going, too."

"The fuck you are, Sandy! He's outside the gate of a loony bin. I'll be lucky if I get to the bottom of the hill before he takes off. Let's take this slow. Do I look pretty?" Hadn't meant to say the last part.

She pulls the barrette from my hair, finger-combs

it and twists it, pinning it back up to my head, and tugs the hem of my skirt straight all around. "Beautiful. Now go before he comes to his senses and leaves."

It's a mile walk down the hill in eleven o'clock sun - not really, but might as well be. If my feet were less tough I know they'd be blistered by the hot asphalt, and progress is slow as I seem to be wading through marshmallow. When I near the guard shack, which looks sorta like a fancy outhouse, I can also see the car, Eddie's El Camino, pulled off the road at the end of the drive.

Max is with him, in sunglasses like pilots in movies wear. He stands between Eddie, who leans like an embarrassed child against the car, and the gate, his head swiveling back and forth between the name of the institution and the blonde kid with his chin tucked.

"Hey, Shane," I wave as I pass. "They're cool. I won't be long."

"Hey!" he calls back, "Bridget! Bridget now, right?"

Shane didn't always work here. I'll leave it at that.

"Yes, Bridget. What?" I hiss.

He points, and I hand him the spade I didn't realize I was still carrying.

And still have half the hill to walk.

Max meets me at the gate, hands circling the bars. "What'd that guy take?"

"My garden spade."

"Why?"

I laugh, wrapping my hands around the bars above his. "It's a weapon."

Silence.

"Hey, Eddie."

He waves reluctantly, gauze taped to the back of his hand where I buried the cigarette. He's stretching it, bandaged after a week, there's a chance he added the bandage this morning, just for me.

Max and I look.

"So this is home?"

Nodding, "Yeah."

"It looks like a castle."

Over my shoulder, all I can see is the top half of the house, the gables, the eaves, the things that make it look harmless to passersby. "My room is in that top tower, to the left. I climbed down my roommate's hair this morning. I wish you could see my garden from here."

"You have a garden?"

"Yep."

"And I can't come in. And you can't come out."

I swing back and forth away from the bars. "You can. But you have to - you know, do paperwork, and interview the....give me these." I lean forward and snatch off his sunglasses. "Let me see your eyes." I press against the bars, fold my hands over his, rubbing his knuckles with my palms, tingling. "Why did you come here? I didn't expect to see you again."

Max leans forward, presses his mouth to my shoulder. His breath runs through the left side of my body. "You smell like sun and dirt."

"And you look like sex. Why are you here?"

"This is Eddie's family's place?"

"Yes, sort of. His great-grandparents built it. It's not my place to tell you this shit."

Without the sunglasses, without the garage, Max is exposed. He doesn't look at my face, he looks down, his eyelashes tell me nothing. "Come see me. Or I'll come see you." He kisses each of my shoulders, my toes curling on one foot then the other. He laces his arms through the bars. "Can you get out of here? Like leave and get an apartment, or something? A job? I don't think you're *that* crazy. There are *bars*." He slips his hands behind my back and pulls me against the bars, locking his mouth to mine, we're warm up through the middle.

"Bridget! Come on!" It's Shane, and I pull back, cheeks warm. "I'm trying to be a nice guy here, but you can't fuck that dude through the gate. Jesus!"

Max opens his mouth and I put my hand over it. "He is being really nice. We're not supposed to touch through the gate at all." He pulls his hands back. "I'm sorry. I want you. But I can't leave. It hasn't even been two years since my last felony. Or two weeks since I was in Neon."

"I don't know what any of that means."

"Every time I leave, I end up back here, anyway. Maybe I am that crazy. But it's okay." I shrug, place my palm flat on his chest. He's warm from the sun. "I wanted to hide this from you, be mysterious and clever. But I want you too much to lie. And I don't do escapes anymore." I pull back my hand, I've left a dirty palm print. "What kind of car are you building in the garage?"

Max runs his hands up my arms, goosebumps. "It's a 1953 Studebaker Starlight Coupe. What's your real name?"

"I'd like to see it when it's finished, all in one piece." With my garden-stinking hands, I cradle his face, and kiss him. At the moment the magnets pull me forward, at the moment I'm afraid, I pull back.

"Your name?"

"The one I had right before this, or the one before that or the one I'll pick after I'm tired of being Bridget?" Quietly, into his ear.

He stiffens. "Your *real* name."

"I don't remember."

"You're a bad liar." Max presses his lips to the concave spot between my collarbones at the base of my throat. If I swallow, he'll feel it, so I don't. His hair smells like shampoo, and a little like motor oil.

"Will you come back?"

He growls into my chest. "I have to, don't I?"

"What about your girlfriend?"

"Gone. I just needed an excuse."

Slipping his sunglasses up on my head, I move his head to kiss him again, but he leans away.

"What felony?"

"I shot Eddie." I look over Max's shoulder. "Sorry, Eddie."

Eddie shrugs, turns his palms to the sky.

"Are you fucking kidding me? That's why you're in

here? Attempted murder?"

"Oh no. I shot him while I was already in here - it's a long story. But no one knows, he never told. I mean, you know, and I know....." I step back, my knees shaky. There's a tightrope floating right inside the gate, I keep losing my balance. "If this is it, just tell me. It's easier than you making promises and never seeing you again."

"Come here," Max reaches through the bars and drags me forward by the wrist, his fingertips desperate enough to bruise. "Mine," he whispers in my ear.

But it's not really an answer.

He walks back to the car without another word, the sunlight drawing a yellow aura along his shoulders and hair. Eddie doesn't look back, either. I wrap my arms around the bars and lean my face against them, watching the El Camino go.

"Thanks, Shane." He hands me back my spade without a word, and I finish my climb.

Sandra, Gerald, Charlotte, and Amy are waiting in a row next to the garden, practically tilted forward in anticipation.

"What now?" Charlotte asks.

"Lunch."

Emma has become part of the family, and her routine is shaping Sandra's routine in ways I hadn't foreseen when I discovered her in the gravel dust. Sandra hasn't had

Dr. Spock out since last week's "incident" - she still reads every morning, but now it's ten year old Family Circle magazines, and she's been working on a paperback romance since last Sunday.

Gerald and Amy reached some sort of weird understanding. After all this time, they began discussing poetry. They exchange books, make lists for the library to order, have been tossing around the idea of a book club. Amy's wearing lipstick. Things are happening.

As we pretty much expected, Charlotte had a little relapse after her mom failed to show. Too smart to sneak out of her room, she'd carefully tapped at one of the windowpanes with a towel-wrapped fist until it had cracked near the frame, removed the shard and proceeded to pretty well remove the pads of four fingers before the 2am bed check. I offered Dr. Matthews everything I could think of, if he'd just talk to her doctor about expediting our roommate request. He agreed to talk to her doctor if I promised never to offer fellatio again.

Charlotte was released from the Neon Ward yesterday and allowed to pack. So, I have a roommate. Who likes Scooby Doo, of all the goddamn things to like. There's a big poster of the Mystery Machine on the back of our door. I didn't have the heart to tell her it was a dumb idea, since we aren't allowed to close our doors. Apparently it's something girls do. How would I know? I'm pushing thirty.

The moon is full. Yvonne lets Charlotte and I sneak out after everyone's gone to bed, provided we stay within sight. I spread a blanket on the grass, and give her one of my last two cigarettes.

We've come to moon bathe. The sky is clear. The stars are like thousands of tiny rabbit holes, a different room in each one, and the moon may be the White Whale, if there ever was one.

I don't tell these things to Charlotte. We lie on our backs and blow smoke rings, the last of the lightning bugs closing up shop for the night. At this moment, we can feel like tiny creatures, unimportant and insignificant in a comforting way.

Charlotte tells me her birthday is on the 4th of July, and I tell her she's lucky, that she has a party every year whether anyone remembers or not.

"It's not so bad here," she says, her black hair spread in a fan above her head. "But I'd just as soon live on the moon, if I could live anywhere. Wouldn't you?"

If I let go of the things I know, I can feel the blanket as a raft beneath us, and the sky floating above. "No. I'd live in the ocean."

"Really?"

I twine my fingers with hers. "Are you kidding? If I could breathe underwater I'd never see any of you again."

Color the manatee pink!

PILFERING LIFE

So, the thing is: I'm thinking and thinking. I was thinking about how I wanted to tell you about when I worked at the saddle shop and the time the big mineral tub (set out for advertisement, so people could see how big it was, plenty big enough to put in the field) got rained in and drew flies and it was right next to the entrance door, and Jerry tried to drag the thing off with a tractor and chain and just succeeded in spilling this sticky mineral molasses sticky mixture of shit over all the concrete step/walk right outside the door, and I watched the whole thing from the door, him dragging it down the gravel drive behind the tractor splashing the shit everywhere and finally getting what was left of it into the barn.

So it's a Monday afternoon, June, gorgeous day, not a customer in sight for the past hour, and it's me and Jerry - he's mid-60s, horse-trader and farmer, the man who wastes nothing and sells everything - seriously, his

brother-in-law gave him two Aussie pups
and he LOVED them, but just the same
sold the pair that afternoon and got $75
for them, then went back to his wife to
see if he could get a couple more - to
keep this time for himself, and surely
he meant it, but she was pissed and it's
true that if someone asked him to buy
the next two he would've sold those,
too, of course she didn't help - and his
wife is Bev, that I used in Trot Lines,
that had the Aussie named Roberta, and
Bev really did have an Aussie named
Roberta - the dog was like fourteen
years old when I worked there and
weighed over 50lbs and had arthritis
and skin problems and took like six
pills a day, and Bev would vacuum
Roberta, like with a vacuum cleaner with
a hose, when Roberta got itching too bad
Bev'd just put the brush attachment on
the hose and put one boot on Roberta's
ass and shove and Roberta would grunt
and stretch out by the door while Bev
vacuumed the itch away - and Bev was
awesome, too, once flicked her cigarette
butt out her pick-up window, it landed
in the back of her truck and set it on
fire, she was going down the highway
with the truck on fire and tried to
dump her beer out the window to put out
the fire - different story, and I heard
like three different versions of what
happened - only thing I know for sure

is the truck DID burn up, she showed me
pictures, think I told you that one.

Anyway, back to Jerry - we're standing
there in our jeans and boots staring at
this small moat of stickiness and he
says "You gonna clean this up?" I just
say "nope" so he goes walking down to
the barn, and I stay outside, you just
never know what's going to happen, and
he comes back out of the barn a couple
minutes later with two horses in halters
and lead ropes and walks up and hands
me one of the leads, and we lead them
to the moat of sweet mineral, and stand
there in the sun, leaning against the
building on this quiet, blue sky, warm
gorgeous perfect amazing afternoon, just
leaning against the building watching
the sky and these two horses cleaning up
(and more importantly NOT WASTING) the
mineral molasses, and Jerry says "You
know you can't tell anybody about this,
right?" and I know he means the tractor,
and the mess, and the horses, and
mainly what could be construed as Not
Working on a perfectly workable summer
afternoon, and I said "Yeah, I know,"
and we stood there quiet for probably an
hour, just soaking in the day and the
quiet and the sun and fields and smell
of the horses and it's easily one of the
most memorable and beautiful afternoons

of my life...

So I'm thinking about THAT, wanting
to tell you about THAT, and then I'm
thinking about this message I got from
Morey that says "Hey whatever happened
with that story about the white trash
stud?" and also I'm thinking about
Trotlines in MH and then I'm reading
this article about misconceptions about
the poor and I'm thinking about voice
and MY voice and the stuff you were
talking about, writing where YOU were
from and Salford and then all the stuff
about me writing my past and all my
FEARS and then I just circle right back
around to this thing about Jerry, this
time at the saddle shop, and what it was
like to run through tobacco fields when
I was little and throwing beer bottles
at road signs from car windows when I
was sixteen, even though I'm wearing
raccoon eyeliner and leopard pumps I'm
still an Appalachian girl, a girl that
NEVER litters, NEVER, but fuck, everyone
knows throwing a beer bottle at a sign
is not littering...

And I think it's finally gotten through.
I have to write this all out. It's all
gotta be fiction, of course, truth
disguised as fiction, but dammit, it all

feels SO CLOSE to the surface, the only
time I ever went mud-running, with my
sister and our friends Tommy and Jason
and - I think I told you the story,
yeah? With the Lost Boys soundtrack
and losing my flip-flop - but anyway,
it's all there - I just have to go drag
Bridget out of The Gilded Cage and make
her be me, but in disguise....

Credits

Hollow Creatures was a conversation with H.R. Tardiff
(Keep your eyes peeled for more of that, we're conspiring.)

The Cabbage Muse originally appeared in cutaway, 2012

Teetotaler originally appeared in Thunderdome, 2011

The World Was Clocks originally appeared in Warmed and
Bound, 2011

Fever originally appeared in Thunderdome, 2012

Gilded Bones originally appeared in
In Search of a City: Los Angeles in 1,000 Words, 2012

Trotlines originally appeared in Menacing Hedge, 2012

Asymmetry originally appeared in Cipher Sisters, 2013

Eight Years Coming was a fake conversation in response to
a throwaway comment by Brien Piechos on a random news
article

Short Tendon originally appeared in
The Booked. Anthology, 2013

The Old Universe originally appeared in
Nefarious Muse, 2011

Pilfering Life was an email to Craig Wallwork

Acknowledgements

Thank you and I love you to the following people, and the people I know I must've forgotten:

Eric, Mike, Craig, Richard, Hilary, Angela, Beth, Chris, Gordon, Boden, Jesse, JR, Amy, Heather, Jon, Robb, Liv, Pete, Gayle, Brien, Sean, Mlaz, Pela, Eddy, Morey, Caleb, DB, Kelly, Grig, Andrea, Lon, everyone I worked with in Cultshop back in the day, Write Club 2011, The Velvet, my uncle Jim for that pile of King books when I was eleven, my parents for reading, my family for trying to keep up, and most of all my son - for telling better stories to me than the ones I tell him.

If you enjoyed this book,
please recommend us to your friends.
As with any mind-altering substance,
sharing is caring.

www.ThunderdomePress.com

CPSIA information can be obtained
at www.ICGtesting.com
Printed in the USA
LVOW10s0222130218
566382LV00013B/396/P